Oct 18	Jl 6 '87	MAR 1 - 1994
NOV 3 1986	J' 25 '87	AUG 1 9 1998
NOV 14 1986	Ag 25 3	
Nov 23	Oc 12 '87	
DEC 19 1986	De 5 '87	DEC 0 5 1999
JAN 30 1987		
Ma 6 '87	Jl 30 '88	
Ap 3 '87	Ag 19 '88	
My 8 '87	Se 15 '90	
Ju 1 '87	OCT 1 4 1996	
	NOV 0 7	

LIGHT THROUGH GLASS

Also by Elizabeth Lemarchand

*Available in Walker paperback

LIGHT THROUGH GLASS

Elizabeth Lemarchand

18342

Walker and Company
New York

To Pat Blyth

London excepted, all places and persons mentioned in this book are entirely the product of the author's imagination.

First published in the United States of America in 1986 by the Walker Publishing Company, Inc.

Library of Congress Cataloging-in-Publication Data

Lemarchand, Elizabeth.
    Light through glass.

    I. Title.
PR6062.E5L5   1986   823'.914   86-7739
ISBN 0-8027-5649-2

Printed in the United States of America

10 9 8 7 6 5 4 3 2 1

F
L

CHIEF CHARACTERS

MINSTOW COLLEGE

William Appleton M.B.E. M.A.	Principal
John Paterson D.Sc. F.R.G.S.	Head of Geography and Geology Department
Ronald Grimshaw	Deputy Head
Mrs Anne Brothers	Departmental Secretary
Bridget Appleton	William's wife
Linda Grimshaw	Ronald's wife

MEMBERS OF PATERSON FAMILY
and EMPLOYEES

Mark Forbes	John's nephew
Grizel Ross	John's aunt
Jean Naylor	Grizel Ross's companion
Mrs Dredge	John's daily

POLICE

Superintendent Lock
Inspector Charles Nevinson   } Minstow
Virginia his wife
Sergeant Andrews

Detective Chief-Superintendent
    Tom Pollard   } New Scotland Yard
Detective-Inspector
    Gregory Toye

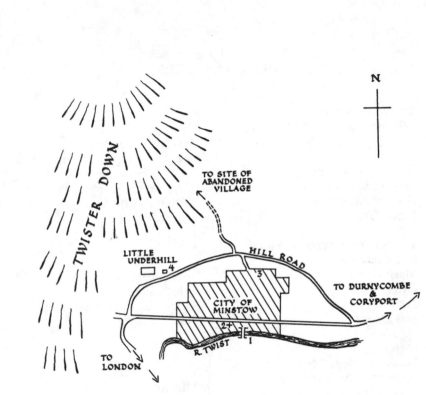

N

TWISTER DOWN

TO SITE OF
ABANDONED
VILLAGE

LITTLE
UNDERHILL

HILL ROAD

3

TO DURNYCOMBE
&
CORYPORT

CITY OF
MINSTOW

4

2

1

R. TWIST

TO
LONDON

1. THE OLD BRIDGE

2. BRIDGE CHAPEL

3. ROSEMARY CLOSE

4. LOYES COTTAGE

PART ONE

Chapter One

The room was of reasonable size with the standard decor and furnishings of a Head of Department's office at the Minstow College of Education. Its current occupant, Dr John Paterson D.Sc. F.R.G.S., was Head of the combined Geology and Geography Department. He had private means, and had introduced a few personal touches indicative of his interests. On the walls were two good oils of mountain landscapes and a barometer in a beautiful mahogany banjo-shaped case. A bronze of a stag on a craggy summit occupied a side table.

At 3.30 on the afternoon of Friday 20 October, John Paterson was sitting at his desk signing his outgoing correspondence. The College was about to disperse for the customary week's break in the middle of the autumn term and he worked quickly and decisively. The job finished, he replaced the letters in a folder, opened a drawer and took out two in his own handwriting. He read them through twice, reflected briefly and finally put them into an envelope which he stuck down and addressed. Finally he buzzed his secretary.

Mrs Anne Brothers came promptly through the door leading to her adjoining office. She was a woman in her early thirties with dark hair worn short and a competent impassive expression.

'Last job before we pack it in,' Paterson said, glancing up and handing her the folder. 'Get this lot off, and this one' – he passed over the addressed envelope – 'is to go to the Principal on Monday week when we start up again. Then get off yourself, my dear. Ted's picking you up with the car, I expect? What time does your plane take off?'

'6.15,' she told him. 'Check-in's 5.15. We've plenty of time, barring accidents. But I'm afraid it's not the last job for you, Dr Paterson. Mr Grimshaw's in my office and says he wants to see you urgently. I told him you were going off on fieldwork first thing tomorrow and were in a hurry to get away, but he said it couldn't wait.'

'Hell!' Paterson jerked up his head and scowled. 'I suppose the Grainger Award Committee's decision must have leaked out. It wasn't supposed to be public property till we got back after the break. Send him in, then, but say I can only give him five minutes and he must look slippy. . . . Have the whale of a week in Majorca.'

'Thank you,' Anne Brothers replied. 'I hope the fieldwork goes well, and the good weather lasts.'

She went out, closing the connecting door into her office.

John Paterson sat on at his desk, a striking-looking man of fifty-four, suntanned and powerfully built, with springy hair once reddish but now greying and beginning to recede from his massive forehead. He was thick-lipped with a big shapely nose. In response to the knock on Anne Brothers' door he gave an irritated shout of 'Come in'.

Ronald Grimshaw, Deputy Head in the Department and in charge of Geography, was fifteen years younger

4

and unremarkable in appearance apart from a good brow and intelligent light grey eyes. He strode up to the desk gripping a copy of the *Minstow Evening News*.

John Paterson stared at him and did not invite him to sit down.

'Well, what is it?' he demanded. 'Can't it wait until after next week? I'm in a hurry to get off. I've all my stuff to collect up for camping out over at Durnycombe.'

'No, it can't wait,' Ronald Grimshaw replied tersely. 'My attention's just been drawn to this.' He held out the newspaper indicating a column heading on the front page: MINSTOW COLLEGE STUDENT GETS PLACE ON EXPEDITION TO MOUNT IOTA. 'And,' Grimshaw went on, 'I've just heard from a reliable source that Billings, obviously the student in question, has been awarded the whole of the Grainger grant for this year.'

'Perfectly correct,' Paterson lounged back in his chair and sat toying with a paper knife. 'So what?'

'Perfectly stagemanaged would be nearer the mark,' Grimshaw retorted, controlling himself with difficulty. 'I taught Billings in his first year and he's no more than good average. But you know the chap who chaired the committee interviewing students for Mount Iota, don't you? Well enough for him to write an introduction to that book of yours. This is supposed to be a joint Geography and Geology Department and I've been kept completely in the dark over the whole business. Do you think I should have let my people sweat blood over their settlement pattern project if I'd known you were running Billings – having sworn him to keep mum, presumably – and that if he got a place, it would be public knowledge on the very day Grainger was being awarded, and ensure that he'd have the cash to go? Obviously he'd get the Grainger. A bloody good boost for the College entirely due to you. The end justifying the means, in short.'

5

Still lounging in his chair, Paterson raised his eyebrows.

'It's fortunate for you that there was no witness to your remarks relating to Professor Gatherson's chairmanship of the Iota selection of students. Had there been, you could quite well have found yourself facing a charge of slander. With regard to Billings, it's my province as Head of the combined Department to assess the nature and quality of the work going on in it. Billings is a promising geologist who submitted a scheme for an on-site investigation of one aspect of the Mount Iota volcanic eruption. Presumably even you would admit that the eruption is a matter of world scientific interest. Your people's proposed study of a settlement pattern in Brittany is hardly in the same category, you know. In any case, don't you think that research into settlement patterns may have been a bit overdone in recent years?'

'If I did,' Grimshaw retorted, 'it wouldn't be part of my students' syllabus. And it will continue to be when I take over the combined Department next year. There'll be some other changes. Your successor who'll be my deputy, as I'm alleged to be yours, will be treated as a colleague, not as a dogsbody, and won't be kept in the dark about what's going on.'

'I beg your pardon?' Paterson tilted his head back and contemplated Grimshaw with malicious satisfaction. 'You're under a misapprehension. I've just sent a letter to the Principal withdrawing my provisional resignation. If you find your own position in the Department unsatisfactory, why not resign yourself? Obviously in these days of staff reductions you're afraid you'd never get another lectureship with your mediocre qualifications. Quite understandably. And one needs referees, doesn't one? The scope you have here is perfectly suited to your capacities.'

Grimshaw stood contemplating him in stunned silence. . . .

'Scum has a way of floating to the top,' he said at last, and made to turn on his heel.

Paterson gave an unpleasant laugh.

'Don't be in such a hurry. I've something also to tell you that you'll find quite interesting.'

A few minutes later as Grimshaw's footsteps died away John Paterson sat on with an expression of satisfied malevolence and pleasurable anticipation on his face. Then he got up, checked the maps and notebooks in his briefcase and made his way to the lift. In the staff car park he came on the Principal, Bill Appleton, with his wife Bridget, on the point of driving off. Greetings were exchanged with outward friendliness.

'You're for France, I hear?' Paterson said.

'We are,' Bill Appleton replied, 'by the night ferry. A family foursome with our daughter and son-in-law.'

'No fixed plans,' Bridget contributed. 'Just tooling around and stopping off when we feel like it. Super, if only this St Luke's summer goes on. What are you doing, Dr Paterson?'

'A local busman's holiday. I've banked on the weather holding and decided to camp in my Caravette for a few days in the Durnycombe Fall area, to do a bit of fieldwork on the cliff formation. There are some interesting discrepancies in the bedding of the sandstones – but I mustn't get technical.'

They wished him luck and started off.

'You've got to hand it to him that he's dead keen on his shop,' Bridget remarked as they waited at traffic lights. 'How good is he? As a geologist, I mean?'

'Quite good, but not top class, of course. He's done some useful bits of research, and gets articles into reputable geological publications. He's just had a book

7

commissioned on coastal features, and he's let it be known that he's putting in for the voluntary redundancy scheme at fifty-five at the end of this academic year. As a human being he's about the most self-centred bastard I've ever come up against.'

'You'd have thought he'd have aimed a bit higher, all things considered. A university job, I mean.'

'His job with us suits him down to the ground. Not too demanding, and plenty of spare time for his own work, and he is an absolute adept at shoving off departmental chores on to his junior, Ronald Grimshaw, who's the geographer and has a dog's life, poor blighter. He'd move if it wasn't so difficult to get a job with current staffing cuts.'

'If Paterson's clearing out at the end of the year will this unfortunate chap get the Department?'

'I'm going to do everything I possibly can to nobble it for him and I think it's in the bag all right. He's well qualified and the students like him, and I feel Paterson's been such a stinker that College owes him something, but as you know we are obliged to advertise our jobs. But even if a real top-notcher applied that we had to have, Grimshaw's whole existence would be transformed.'

A few minutes later Bill Appleton turned in at the south gateway of Minstow's Cathedral Close, and drew up outside the small eighteenth-century house of their friends the Nevinsons for a quick cup of tea en route for the ferry. Some years earlier Virginia Gould, as she then was, had bought a cottage next door to the Appletons' in the nearby village of Marleigh. It was here that she had met Detective-Inspector Charles Nevinson while he was investigating a local case of murder and arson.

Tea was waiting for them round a welcoming log fire. Bridget and Virginia were quickly absorbed in Roland

Nevinson aged eleven months, awake and perky after his afternoon sleep. Bill Appleton put down a half-empty cup and surveyed the trio appreciatively. It struck him as it often had before what an interesting contrast they presented: Bridget, fifteen years the elder, robust and buoyant with her mop of curly hair and glowing sunburn, and Virginia, slight and small, with sleek dark hair and clear attractive pallor. Hardly surprising, Bill thought, recalling with indignation the calculated vindictiveness of her cousin Nigel Kerslake over their uncle's bequest to her of his house and its contents.

He picked up his cup, drained it and turned to Charles Nevinson, a tall, dark man sprawling comfortably in an armchair, his long legs stretched out to the log fire.

'How goes it at the station?' he asked.

Charles grinned.

'Peaceful. A bit on the quiet side, perhaps. Motoring offences, minor break-ins, Saturday night breaches of the peace, a suspected arson . . .'

'Here,' Bill said, 'you're not thinking of putting in for a transfer to a livelier spot, are you?'

Charles made a comprehensive gesture taking in his wife, son and surroundings.

'Not for the present, anyway. We like the house immensely and being here in the Close, and the chaps down at the station are a great bunch, the Super included.'

'You've been lucky there. Some blokes might feel a bit hipped at a mere Inspector having got to know Detective-Chief Superintendent Pollard of New Scotland Yard over the Marleigh case. . . . Give that brat back to its Mum, Biddy, and let's get cracking or we'll miss the ferry.'

*   *   *

With their departure from the College car park the Appletons dropped out of John Paterson's mind. He walked to his Chrysler, ran an appreciative eye over its immaculate coachwork and took out his car keys. He lived in bachelor comfort at Little Underhill, a village on the outskirts of Minstow which was progressively absorbing it. His tile-hung cottage in a cul-de-sac faced south over the few remaining fields and coppices. On arrival he drove into an adjoining barn which he had converted into an integral garage, and parked beside the Caravette which he used for camping on his geological expeditions. On going through into the cottage he encountered agreeable warmth and a faint combined scent of furniture polish and chrysanthemums. His daily woman, a Mrs Dredge from the village, had learnt to achieve his exacting standards over the maintenance of Loyes Cottage and was paid proportionately highly. He carried out a tour of inspection to his complete satisfaction. The small spare room showed no sign of having been occupied overnight. Closing the door he went downstairs again, reflecting on the pleasure of having his home to himself again. Frankly it was a damn nuisance that Iremonger Properties, the London estate agency for which his nephew worked, seemed to send him so often to the Minstow locality to inspect properties and interview prospective clients. It wasn't much more than a month ago that he'd wanted a bed for a night. The Crown in Minstow was quite a decent pub. Why couldn't he stay there at Iremonger's expense? Still, admittedly, that particular visit had paid off. . . .

John Paterson's thoughts turned to the pleasing prospect of a pot of Lapsang Souchon, and he went to brew one in his small but admirably equipped kitchen. He returned to the sitting-room carrying the teatray left in readiness by Mrs Dredge, and settled himself comfortably in an armchair with the day's *Times*. Before tackling the leader he sat for a couple of minutes sipping with enjoyment and relishing the memory of his recent conversation with Ronald Grimshaw.

He had just poured himself a second cup when the telephone bleeped. He swore, and flung down the *Times* as he went to answer it. To his surprise the caller was Mark Forbes.

'I'm in a bit of a jam, Uncle John,' he heard. 'The two jobs on the far side of Coryport took much longer than I expected, and I was belting along to get home at a reasonable hour when a bloody stone flew up and shattered my windscreeen. I had to crawl to a one-eyed show called Grey's Garage, about ten miles from Minstow, and they say they can't get hold of a replacement and fix it much before 10 tomorrow morning. So I wondered if I could land myself on you again for tonight? The chap here can hire me a Mini of some sort and I'd like to come in and collect you for some dinner at the Crown if you'd care for that.'

Annoyance at having his evening disrupted competed in John Paterson's mind with the advantage of a tolerably good meal at Mark's – or probably Mark's Company's – expense, and no trouble to himself.

'Well, there's a bed here if you want one,' he replied, 'but not much food in the house as I'm off first thing tomorrow as you know. So it's definitely a case of eating out if you come.'

'Fine,' Mark Forbes replied. 'And thanks a lot. I'll clear off when you do tomorrow, so the Dredge needn't have the shock of finding me around. OK if I turn up about half-past six? I've got to wait for the Mini to come back from somewhere. This is a pretty small-scale set-up.'

'You'll find me here,' John Paterson replied. 'All

right, then.' He brought the conversation to an end by replacing the receiver, reflecting as he did so that since Mark's visit in September he had found him better company.

As he expected the cup of tea was by now tepid and undrinkable, and he decided that the contents of the pot would be stewed. Returning the tray to the kitchen he began to assemble his spare kit, equipment and supplies for the following morning and transfer them to the Caravette in the garage.

After John Paterson had driven away in his Chrysler the College buildings had progressively emptied and silence had taken over. Synchronised electric clocks jolted one minute after another into oblivion. Unconscious of the passage of time Ronald Grimshaw sat on at his desk staring unseeingly in front of him. After some time he realised that his hands were hurting him and relaxed his unconscious grip on a half-open drawer. Slowly, the realisation of the full implications of John Paterson's cancelled resignation gave way to devasting fury and sheer hatred toward him. The unconcealed contempt and cavalier treatment of himself and his students which he had endured over the past five years was not, after all, coming to an end in the near future. Far from it. And all this was dwarfed by the fact that somehow Paterson had learnt something enabling him to exercise a cashless but lethal form of blackmail. Without warning the situation exploded in Grimshaw's mind into a lurid vision of executing crude physical violence on Paterson, bloody and humiliating. . . .

'Beg pardon, sir. I didn't know you was still around.'

'Just finishing off a job, Barnett. I'll clear out in five minutes.'

'No need to 'urry yourself, sir. I'll check the top floor an' then come back 'ere.'

The porter vanished, Extraordinary, Grimshaw thought, how you could switch from fantasy back into reality in a split second. He hastily collected up some books and papers, stuffed them into his case and made tracks for the lift to avoid any further conversation with Barnett.

Outside dusk was falling and there was a nip of frost in the air. Luminous haze hung about the street lamps. He had not intended to be out so late and shivered slightly in his light pullover as he strode homewards. A thought detached itself from the tumult in his mind and brought an unexpected sense of relief. At least Linda, his wife, was away on a visit to a former office colleague until Sunday evening. He would not have to face her reactions to Paterson's cancelled departure for forty-eight hours. If – improbably – she rang tonight he would manage to keep off the subject somehow. . . .

Home was a small modern house on a new estate, Rosemary Close, some ten minutes from the College. As he let himself in it felt stuffy and dead. Moving like an automaton he mixed himself a whisky and soda and took it into the lounge, drawing the curtains, switching on the electric fire and slumping down into an armchair.

After a time his eyes fell on his wife's photograph. He sat gazing at the vital little face with just that hint of wariness about the mouth, the ineradicable outward sign of an upbringing in an orphanage, albeit an enlightened and caring one. A naturally protective man himself it was through this streak of vulnerability that he had been attracted to her in the first place. After their marriage it had impelled him to work for the professional advancement that would bring them the assured social status she craved and a larger income.

13

When the promising appointment to Minstow College had turned out so disastrously Linda's sympathy and support had been the one thing that had made it possible to endure life under Paterson. Then, soon after the beginning of the current term, had come that incredible sunburst: Paterson's announcement of his intention to resign at the end of the academic year and accept the voluntary redundancy offer to any member of staff willing to go at the age of fifty-five. This barely credible news had been followed by a summons to the Principal, and the virtual guarantee of the succession to the headship of the department.

Now, in just forty-eight hours' time, Linda would have to be told that they had merely been spending a brief interval in a fools' paradise. . . . Perhaps, Grimshaw wondered, that bastard Paterson had never meant to clear out. . . . Had it been simply a bit of his bloody sadism, just for the hell of it? Like this afternoon's.

Framing tentative sentences with which to break the news of the cancelled resignation to Linda he sat on, finally abandoning the attempt and letting unco-ordinated thoughts of a hopeless nature drift through his mind.

Ultimately he was roused by a ring at the front door bell and struggled to his feet. A near neighbour was on the step, Jim Biden, a cheerful uncomplicated engineer.

'I say, your wife's away, isn't she? Come over right now and take pot luck with us. Oh, come off it man,' he insisted. 'You can't possibly have a lot of urgent work on hand with a week's holiday ahead, you lucky devil. Pam says it's her idea and you simply must come.'

Suddenly feeling that anything would be preferable to a solitary evening of reliving the conversation with Paterson and looking ahead to Linda's return, Ronald Grimshaw accepted.

14

'It's jolly decent of you,' he said. 'I'm a rotten cook and had resigned myself to bread and cheese. I'll be along in ten minutes. OK?'

After the trauma of the past hours he found the cheerful ordinariness of the Bidens' home soothing and even enjoyable. It was past 11 when he got up to go.

A couple of minutes later while unlocking his front door he abruptly swung round, aware of a figure coming quietly and swiftly towards him from the side of the house.

Chapter Two

The fine still weather lasted on into the following week. On the morning of Thursday, 26 October, a small commercial helicopter took off from an airfield near Coryport, fifty miles west of Minstow. It was piloted by Jim Waldron, an employee of Surefly Limited, and also carried Reg Brand, a professional photographer. It headed for the coast.

'I take it you want to go in close to the cliffs to get your pictures?' Waldron asked.

'That's the idea. I've been hired by a bloke at Minstow College who's writing a book about the coastline.'

As the helicopter proceeded purposefully through the calm bright air they agreed that it was just the day for the job now that the early morning mist had cleared, and the programme was carried out as planned. Brand studied a succession of cliff faces through binoculars, and at intervals told Waldron to hold it while he took a series of photographs with a varied assortment of cameras.

'Blimey,' Waldron remarked after a time. 'I've never been right in close before. Looks like the sort of thing you see in a nightmare, doesn't it?'

It was an apt comparison. The formidable cliffs rose sheer from sea level to nearly 1000 feet. Over aeons of geological time layers of sediments had been formed under the sea and then slowly and relentlessly thrust up, and buckled in the process into huge crazy folds progressively compressed, fractured, and forced one over the other. At the foot of the tremendous bastion jagged rock pinnacles reared out of the water indicating the former extension of the coastline. At intervals the misty white ribbons of waterfalls hung apparently motionless in ravines cut deep in the cliff face, their impact with the sea inaudible through the drone of the helicopter's engine.

Brand, absorbed in technical problems, gave a grunt of assent as he feverishly switched from one piece of his equipment to another and focussed lenses.

'Pull out just a bit, will you?' he said a few moments later. 'This chap's the star turn: Durnycombe Fall. I want to get the reflection in the stretch of calm water at the bottom. . . . Thanks. That's spot on. . . . Wonderful what a bit of glass will do for you.'

At this point on the coast rock pinnacles partly enclosed a small bay into which the spectacular waterfall precipitated itself in a mass of foaming whiteness. Beyond this ever-renewed tumult the greenish-blue sea water was gently ruffled in an ebbing tide, creaming round the bases of the stacks. Brand suddenly broke off from muttering to himself about light effects and shadows.

'God!' he exclaimed, 'there's a van or something half under the water down there! Look – over on the left, wedged between a couple of those rocks. Take us back in a bit, can you?'

'You're dead right,' Waldron confirmed a few moments later. 'How the heck did it get there? Must've come over the top. Being washed along the coast would've broken it up.'

17

'Anybody inside the thing, I wonder? . . . If there is he'll have had it all right, poor bastard.'

The possibility of having discovered a fatal accident reminded Waldron of his official status as the helicopter's pilot.

'It's back to base right now to put in a report,' he said. 'Sorry, mate, if you haven't got all the shots you wanted.'

Detective-Inspector Charles Nevinson was on the point of leaving Minstow police station for his home and lunch when he was summoned to his Super's office.

Superintendent Lock, a man of fifty with a cheerful reddish face and shrewd blue eyes, looked up from his desk as Nevinson came in.

'Sorry about this when you're just due for a spell of off-duty,' he said, picking up a slip of paper, 'but with Tomlinson on that Westleigh burglary and Reeves off sick it has to be your pigeon. This is a report from the Surefly people which has just come in. About an hour ago one of their chaps was piloting a helicopter along the Durnycombe cliffs for a bloke to take some photographs when they spotted a small van half-submerged in the water. As far as they could make out there was nobody inside. They think it must have come over the cliff. However there's been no report of an accident so far. Over to you, anyway.'

'I suppose it could have been a lone holiday-maker with no fixed programme,' Nevinson commented. 'Royal Naval Air Station at Gatherfield, I take it, sir? Get them to send out one of their helicopters and winch a man down to have a proper look. Meanwhile I'll contact the Coastguard Rescue Service, and go out to the top of the cliff with Sergeant Andrews, if I can have him,

18

and see if there's any sign of something having happened up there.'

Superintendent Lock agreed that these were the obvious preliminary steps, and added that he would be on hand all the afternoon.

Back in his own room Nevinson rang Virginia who was by now well accustomed to frequent disruptions of her domestic routine, and put through calls to Gatherfield and the headquarters of the Coastguard Rescue Service. Then after a couple of sandwiches and a cup of coffee, he set off for the Durnycombe area driven by Sergeant Andrews. As an afterthought PC Bragg, a photographer, was included in the party.

They followed the main Minstow-Coryport road for some ten miles and then took a narrow lane to their left. This soon petered out into a rutted grass-grown track, and they stopped to inspect the surface. It was hard and dry as a result of the current spell of late summer weather, and unpromising from the point of view of tyre tracks or footprints. Their sole discovery over the next hundred yards was a faint impression of a tyre on a patch of bare earth, too superficial for a cast to be made of it. After Bragg had taken a couple of photographs they walked on and finally came out into an open space at the top of the cliffs. It was roughly eight yards wide, sloping almost imperceptibly seawards for about five yards and then dropping sharply to the cliff edge. The ground cover was matted withered heather and dead bracken interspersed with stunted shrubs and clumps of rank grass. Just above the break of slope there were intermittent traces of the Regional Coastal Path.

'Not much hope of picking up the tracks of a small van on this,' Nevinson said as he surveyed the foreground. 'Short of a tank going over it this sort of stuff would just bounce up again. But if the van thing went over the edge there's bound to be some sign of it.'

They advanced cautiously, doing the last few feet on their stomachs and finding the evidence they were looking for. On the extreme edge there was recently loosened earth showing blurred tyre prints and some torn grass and bracken. The three men peered down into the cleft in which the stream emerged which was to develop into the spectacular Durnycombe Fall. In falling the vehicle had half uprooted a bramble bush and ricocheted to the opposite side of the cleft, gouging out vegetation and pieces of rock before continuing on its headlong descent.

Suddenly the engine of an approaching helicopter was audible.

'Damn!' Nevinson exclaimed. 'We just can't see the bottom from here and what they're doing. Anyway, photograph the damage here, Bragg, while Sarge and I nose round further back. And for God's sake look out for yourself.'

Unexpectedly helped by the slanting rays of the afternoon sun, they picked out enough bent blades of grass and snapped-off fronds of bracken to show that a vehicle had recently crossed the level ground. They continued in a roughly straight line to the spot where PC Bragg was engaged in photography at the edge of the cliff. Under Nevinson's direction Sergeant Andrews drove in pegs to mark the route. They stood back to survey the result of his work.

'Rum, wouldn't you say, sir?' he asked.

'Decidedly rum,' Nevinson agreed. 'A bee-line to the edge, and not a sign of any sort of car having been parked up here on the level bit for any length of time, and perhaps left in neutral and with the brake off. We know all right how careless people are. Let's have another look, though, in case we've missed a bit of litter which might be a lead.'

They crawled on hands and knees over the heather and bracken but found nothing but a couple of disintegrating cigarette ends and the remains of a plastic bag which had once contained crisps. PC Bragg who had joined them was told to photograph the pegs and the finds *in situ*. As he did so the helicopter's engines roared into life and they watched it go out to sea, turn, and head for its base at Gatherfield.

'They'll have winched a chap down to have a proper look, I reckon,' Sergeant Andrews said. 'They'll need special gear to get the van up, though, and take it somewhere for examination.'

PC Bragg volunteered the remark that the way the van seemed to have headed for the top of the cliff looked like suicide to him.

'It's a possibility,' Nevinson agreed. 'One of several. Well, we've done all we can here for the moment and had better get back to base and wait for a phone call from Gatherfield.'

They arrived almost simultaneously with a report from the Royal Naval Air Station. The van had been identified as a white Caravette in a severely damaged condition. The windscreen and windows were smashed and both doors had burst open and were hanging on broken hinges. The interior was awash with a variety of equipment and clothing floating about, but it could be stated categorically that there was no body inside, nor in the vicinity of the wreckage. The front number plate was still attached: ZF2010YT. Police instructions were being awaited before salvage operations were put in hand. The opinion of the member of the helicopter crew who had inspected the wreckage was that the van had been in the water for several days so an appreciable amount of seaweed and other marine debris had drifted into it.

Nevinson seized on the vital point that the van's

number plate carried a local registration number but, before he had time to contact the vehicle licensing department a call came through from the area's Coastguard Headquarters. As he expected, he was told that it was impossible to start on the precipitous descent of the Durnycombe cliffs bordering the Fall so late in the day, but that an experienced rescue squad would begin the descent at first light. A lookout would be kept along the coastline. He rang off and asked the station's switchboard operator to put him through to the car licensing authority. This was a matter of barely a minute, and he was assured that his enquiry would receive immediate attention.

Waiting for a reply he thankfully gulped down a cup of tea while his mind moved ahead to the steps to be taken once the identity of the Caravette's owner had been established. Once again the situation struck him as odd. If the owner of the thing was still alive why hadn't he reported its loss? Could it have been stolen while he was away and taken on a joy ride by an inexperienced driver who had left the brake off, managed to leap out, and then made himself scarce after the Caravette had gone over the cliff? This seemed a credible possibility. On the other hand –

His desk telephone bleeped, cutting into further speculation. A moment later a brisk voice informed him that ZF2010YT was the registration number of a white Caravette, the property of Dr J.R. Paterson of Loyes Cottage, Little Underhill, Minstow.

'Thanks for your prompt service,' he said briefly, putting down the receiver. The name had produced an instant link-up in his mind with Minstow College. Surely Bill Appleton had mentioned a lecturer named Paterson? A further call, this time to the College, produced the information that the Little Underhill address was Dr Paterson's, the Head of the Geography and Geology Department. Nevinson asked for his telephone number, and told the station switchboard operator to ring it. After a full minute the latter reported that there had been no reply.

'OK,' Nevinson said. 'Pack it in.'

As he had sat waiting he was planning his next move. Summoning Sergeant Andrews he briefed him on the results of the enquiries made up to date.

'Go over to Little Underhill as quickly as you can make it,' he said. 'If you can't get an answer at Loyes Cottage try to find out something about Paterson's movements since the College half-term holiday started at the end of the afternoon of the 20th. A daily woman, or anyway somebody who comes in at intervals to keep the place clean would be the best bet. Try the pub: it's coming up to opening time. There's almost sure to be someone there who knows about Paterson's domestic set-up. When you've run whoever it is to earth, don't give any details, of course. Just say that his Caravette has been found smashed up and we want to contact him. Pick up any useful bit of info you can, and then get back here.'

Sergeant Andrews departed. Nevinson's next step was to send a constable out to Durnycombe to wait near the spot at which the Caravette had gone over the cliff in case Paterson turned up after all. It was just possible that he had met another geologist and they had gone off together to some different area along the coast. But surely Paterson would have returned to his camping area by now? It was past 6 o'clock and almost dark.

On enquiry he learnt that Superintendent Lock was free and went along to report developments up to date. To his surprise he found the Chief Constable, Major Waller, with the Super. The CC with whom he had had

23

contacts over the Marleigh case greeted him pleasantly, having a high opinion of his ability and career prospects.

'Got on to anything over this Durnycombe affair, Nevinson?' he asked.

'The van's a Caravette belonging to Dr John Paterson of the College, sir.'

Both Major Waller and the Super exclaimed.

'Good God!' the former said. 'Was he in it?'

'No, sir, RNAS Gatherfield sent out a helicopter and a man was winched down. There's no sign of a body, but the Caravette's badly smashed and apparently anyone driving it could have been thrown out as it crashed down the cliff. I inspected the area on the top and the point where it went over is perfectly obvious. I took PC Bragg and he photographed the place, and also the traces of its route across the top of the cliff to this point.'

'The helicopter chap found the number plate, I take it?' Superintendent Lake asked.

'Yes, sir. I checked with the car licensing people and the College. I've also sent Sergeant Andrews out to the address they gave me to find out if and when Dr Paterson went off in the Caravette and what his plans were. He –Andrews – ought to be back in about an hour from now. I've also contacted the Coastguard Service, and they're sending a rescue squad down the cliff as soon as it's light enough tomorrow. Gatherfield are standing by for instructions from us about retrieving the wreckage. And I sent PC Willis out to Durnycombe in case Dr Paterson turns up expecting to find his bus where he left it.'

'You seem to have covered the ground pretty adequately,' Major Waller said. 'I don't think there's anything further we can do until Andrews gets back, do you, Super?'

'No, sir, I don't. It may turn out that Paterson's away

and somebody pinched the van. Premature to start contacting his relatives.'

Major Waller agreed.

'There's the possibility that he's committed suicide, I suppose, thought it isn't a method I'd choose myself. Well, we've got people to supper tonight and I'm late already. Ring me at home if there are any important developments.'

While this conversation was in progress Sergeant Andrews had arrived at Little Underhill and been directed to Loyes Cottage. He turned down the cul-de-sac in which it stood, and sat for a moment registering its relative seclusion before getting out and ringing the doorbell. There was no answer and no sound of movement inside or of a light in any window. He flashed a torch through a front window and got an impression of a decidedly cushy set up in apple-pie order. Access to the rear of the cottage was barred by a locked garden door. Also locked was the wide door of a windowless extension of the cottage, presumably used as a garage. Having satisfied himself that either no one was at home or that he was not going to be admitted he turned his car and headed for the village pub.

A few patrons were already installed and listened with interest to his conversation with the landlord who was standing behind the bar. He put out a story of Dr Paterson's car having been found some distance away badly smashed up, and how the police were trying to contact its owner who seemed to be away from home. Was there anybody in Little Underhill who went in to clean for Dr Paterson who might know where he could be found?

'Mrs Dredge, that's who does for him,' the landlord

said. 'Four doors down from here on the right. She'll know, if anybody does. . . . Garage been broke into and the van stolen, I take it? 'Appens all the time these days.'

In the general conversation that broke out Andrews managed to extricate himself without giving a direct answer, but not before noting that little personal sympathy for Dr Paterson was being expressed.

His knock on the fourth door down the street was answered by a small neat woman whom he placed in her early sixties. Still grasping the handle she looked at him doubtfully.

'Mrs Dredge?' he asked politely. 'I think you work at Loyes Cottage for Dr Paterson, don't you? The landlord from the Three Crowns sent me along. I'm Sergeant Andrews from Minstow. Here's my identity card for you to see. . . . I'm afraid Dr Paterson's van has been found damaged, and we want to get in touch with him. Can you help us?'

She stood listening to him with oddly downcast eyes.

'Please to step inside,' she said abruptly with a quick glance at neighbouring front doors, and led the way into a small scrupulously neat kitchen. They sat down facing each other across the table, and he briefly described the sighting of the Caravette at the foot of Durnycombe Fall, and put forward the suggestion that Dr Paterson might have gone off and forgotten to put the brake on.

'He never!' Mrs Dredge broke in emphatically with a swift upward glance. 'He'd never do a thing like that, Dr Paterson wouldn't. I've never known a man so careful. More like it was vandals comin' along. He'd 'ave locked up for sure, but the likes of them'd break the van open soon as look at you an' push it over the cliff.'

'We've thought of vandals, Mrs Dredge,' Andrews assured her, 'and of course we'll be making a lot of

26

enquiries. But we want to be quite sure if Dr Paterson did go off in the van himself, and if he did, when it was.'

'Last Saturday morning 'twas. Early, meanin' to camp in the van if the weather 'eld up so as to give 'im more time for lookin' at the rocks for a book he's writin'. An' his nephew – Mr Mark Forbes, that is –must've gone along with 'im, as far as the garage where 'e'd left his car for repairs of some sort the night before. Neither of 'em was at the cottage when I went over to work half-past nine last Saturday mornin'.

'His nephew?' Andrews queried with interest.

'That's right. 'E works for a firm of 'ouse agents up to London, an' they sometimes sends him down this way to look at places. Thursday night – week ago tonight –'e stayed at the cottage, but Dr Paterson said in the note I found at home Saturday mornin' that Mr Mark'd come back for Friday night because of somethin' wrong with 'is car, which he'd left at a garridge out on the Coryport road, and that the spare room'd want doin' out again. Particular, Dr Paterson is. He'll be real put out that they'd taken each other's cameras by mistake. Mr Mark only found out after they'd parted company, and 'e came back 'ere and dropped in Dr Paterson's on 'is way back. About quarter to eleven, 'twas, last Saturday.'

Andrews asked her if she knew Mark Forbes's address or telephone number, and heard that the number would be in the book by the telephone for sure. Dr Paterson was always careful to have everything in order and up-to-date. She'd got the key and they could go over and look it up if the police wanted it. He promptly accepted the offer and drove her round in his car. There was still no sign of life in the cottage. She unlocked the front door, switched on the light and led the way into a fair-sized sitting room.

One thing stood out a mile, Andrews thought as he

27

looked around. There was no shortage of money in this set-up. He took in the deep pile of the carpet, the opulent armchairs and well-filled bookcases, and what looked like being the last word in a telly. A faint aroma of expensive cigar smoke lingered in the air.

Mrs Dredge lost no time in hurrying over to the telephone and consulting a leather-bound notebook beside it.

''Ere 'tis,' she said. 'Forbes, Mark.'

Andrews made a note of the number and while doing so decided on a touch of flattery. It often took people off their guard and led to unexpected bits of info coming out.

'My word,' he said, handing back the notebook and glancing about him. 'You do keep this place a treat.'

Mrs Dredge showed signs of satisfaction.

'It's the same top to bottom. Real particular about the way the place is kept, Dr Paterson is, just as I said. That's why I'll never come to believe 'e'd go off leavin' the van without its brake on good an' proper. Vandals 'twas, you mark my word, and I 'opes you gets 'em. Mind you, Dr Paterson pays well. Always the same 'tis, whether 'e's 'ome or away, and I works just the same. Monday, Tuesday an' Wednesday regular and when 'e wants me extra. I went right through the 'ole place and did out the kitchen cupboards. Swep' out the garridge, too, what's more.'

Andrews' heart sank. If there had been anything in Loyes Cottage relevant to the curious situation at Durnycombe all trace of it would have gone for good and all as the result of this orgy of cleaning.

'Well, Mrs Dredge,' he said, 'thanks a lot for all your help, especially for the phone number. Mr Mark Forbes may very well know what his uncle's plans were as they went off together last Saturday morning. I must get back to report what you've told me to Inspector Nevinson. Could be Dr Paterson's rung in by now.'

He got another quick upward glance, protracted enough for him to recognise dismay rather than distress.

'I only 'opes so,' she said. 'Eight years I've bin workin' for 'im. As jobs go it's a good 'un.'

Andrews cast about in his mind for another opening gambit which might lead to further useful information.

'Is Dr Paterson a widower?' he asked casually as he rose to go.

'Not 'im,' Mrs Dredge replied with an audible snort. 'When 'e goes Mr Mark gets the lot. Tied up on 'im, 'tis, by Dr Paterson's father's Will. All the same, Mr Mark's attentive to 'is uncle. I'll grant you that. Down 'ere only a month ago, 'e was. 'Is own marriage 'as broke up.'

Andrews extricated himself and drove back to police headquarters as fast as he dared.

'You've been the hell of a time,' Nevinson said. 'Got on to anything? There's no news of Paterson.'

As they made for Superintendent Lock's office Andrews admitted to having picked up one or two possible leads. He gave his superiors a careful factual account of his interview with Mrs Dredge.

'I don't doubt,' the Super said thoughtfully, 'that the nephew will confirm everything the Dredge woman says about last Friday night and Saturday morning. You'd better try to get on to him right away, Nevinson. What's your immediate reaction to this gen Andrews has brought back?'

'Assuming Paterson's dead, it seems to me that we're much where we were, sir. Accident through carelessness or sheer bad driving a bit less likely after all Mrs Dredge said about him being such a careful chap. Mark Forbes has an obvious motive on paper for bumping off his uncle which we can put into cold storage pro tem.'

'I think that's my own reaction,' Superintendent Lock said. 'All right. Get yourself put through to Mark Forbes's number and I'll follow on the extension. You can go off, Andrews. You did a useful job.'

'Thank you, sir,' Andrews replied, and withdrew as Nevinson began dialling.

After a rather prolonged spell of the ringing tone a man's voice sounding irritated gave the Forbes number. In the background were the characteristic noises of an informal party in progress.

'Mr Mark Forbes?' Nevinson enquired.

'Speaking.'

'This is Inspector Nevinson of the Minstow police, Mr Forbes. I'm sorry to tell you that the Caravette belonging to your uncle, Dr John Paterson, has been found smashed up at the foot of the Durnycombe cliffs, about twenty-five miles from here. There was no sign of Dr Paterson and we've heard nothing from him.'

Sounds of utter incredulity came over the line.

'I simply can't believe it! I mean, he's about the world's most careful driver. I mean, are you sure it's *his* Caravette?'

'Absolutely sure, Mr Forbes. One of the number plates is still attached to the wreckage.'

Bursts of distant hilarity were audible, and Mark Forbes swore.

'Hold on, will you, while I shut a door on this bloody racket?'

A door slammed and the conversation was resumed.

'When on earth did this happen?' Mark Forbes demanded.

'At the moment we don't know,' Nevinson told him, 'but from the amount of seaweed that's drifted inside the Caravette through the smashed windows and broken doors it must have been several days ago.'

30

'But if my uncle hasn't reported it, surely it must mean that – that – '

'That he didn't survive? Well, I'm afraid it's beginning to look like that, Mr Forbes, and that's why we've contacted you as you're the only member of his family we know of at the moment. And according to Mrs Dredge of Little Underhill, you may have had a lift from Dr Paterson last Saturday morning when he started off for Durnycombe before 9.30 when she came to work. We understand that your own car was in dock at a garage on the Coryport road for a minor repair. Is this correct?'

'Yes and no. Sorry, that sounds idiotic, but really all this is a bit of a shake-up . . . I'll go back a bit. I spent last Thursday night at Loyes Cottage, and went on to inspect a couple of properties on the far side of Coryport on Friday morning. I work for Iremonger Properties. My idea was to drive straight back here as soon as I was through with the job on Friday afternoon. But about halfway between Coryport and Minstow a stone flew up and shattered my windscreen. I managed to wrap a rag round my hand and make a big enough hole to see through, and crawled to a garage I'd noticed on the way out. It's a small show – Grey's Garage – and they said they couldn't get a replacement screen and fix it before about 10 the next morning. So I rang my uncle and asked if he'd put me up for another night. Grey's hired me a spare Mini they have and I got to Little Underhill about half past six. My uncle was going off himself the next morning and there wasn't much food around, so I took him out to dinner at the Crown in Minstow. At least he actually drove us there in his Chrysler. Next morning we started off at the same time, about ten past nine, but I was in the Mini, not with him in the Caravette.'

'You both took the main Minstow – Coryport road, I suppose?' Nevinson asked, feeling his way.

'That's right. I got a bit ahead in the Mini, and was talking to the chap at Grey's Garage when he drove past.'

'And was that the last time you saw Dr Paterson?'

'Yes. When I was through at Grey's I drove to Durnycombe where he was going to work and camp but there was no sign of him or of the Caravette. There's no road along the cliffs, just a rough footpath, so I came to the conclusion that he must have realised during the drive from Minstow that he'd forgotten something vital like a tin-opener, and decided to go to Coryport to get one before setting up camp.'

'What made you go on to Durnycombe yourself?' Nevinson asked, trying to keep the interest he felt out of his voice.

'It was quite infuriating. When I was shifting my things from the Mini to my Jag, I found I'd got Uncle John's camera instead of my own. They're both expensive makes with very similar cases. He uses his for his geological work, and I use mine – it's my firm's, actually – when I'm inspecting properties. The obvious thing was to catch him straight away and change them over.'

'Did you get out of your car when you arrived at Durnycombe?'

'Oh yes. It was rather pointless,. I suppose, as he obviously wasn't there, but I had a good look in both directions, and then hopped into my bus again and started off. I felt I couldn't possibly leave a valuable camera lying about on a public footpath, so decided that the most sensible thing was to drop it in at Loyes Cottage and tell Mrs Dredge what had happened.'

'If possible,' Nevinson said after a brief pause, 'I'd like you to try and fix the times of the various things that took place that Saturday morning. To start with, at what time did you and Dr Paterson leave Loyes Cottage?'

'Just after 9. I can't be more exact than that.'

'Did you travel in convoy, so to speak?'

'I soon pulled ahead as the Mini was faster than the Caravette. I got to Grey's Garage at twenty to ten. I remember noticing the time as I arrived and hoping they'd finished the job, which they had, actually.'

'As you were ahead of Dr Paterson did you notice him passing the garage, or did he stop and get out to have a word with you?'

'He just raised a hand as he drove past, but didn't stop.'

'So that was the last time you saw him?'

'Yes, yes, *yes*. I've already told you that he wasn't anywhere to be seen when I arrived at Durnycombe and that I drove straight back to Loyes Cottage to leave his camera.'

'I know that all these questions are very irritating, Mr Forbes, but the fact remains that at some point after you saw Dr Paterson drive past Grey's Garage his Caravette went over the cliff. Naturally we shall be making enquiries about his possible journey in it to and from Coryport, and it would help to know as nearly as possible when he passed the garage, and how long after that you yourself arrived at Durnycombe.'

'Obviously I can't tell you to the minute. I was talking to the bloke who runs the garage and getting out my cheque book and credit card when the Caravette went past. Say a quarter to ten. When I'd written the cheque and started moving my gear into my Jag I found I'd got the wrong camera and started at once for Durnycombe as I said. Say I got there about five past ten. It's no distance. . . . Look here, Inspector, if there's still no news of my uncle by tomorrow morning, I'd better come down, hadn't I?'

'What other near relatives are there?'

33

'None, really, except his old aunt of eighty-three who lives up in Northshire. She isn't gaga by any means, but I'm sure you'll agree that anyone of her age oughtn't to be worried unless it's absolutely necessary. What moves will you people be making next?'

Nevinson outlined the various searches of the Durnycombe area that would begin at first light on the following morning, and it was agreed that, unless contacted, Mark Forbes should drive down after a brief call at his company's office.

Replacing the receiver, Nevinson looked enquiringly at Superintendent Lock.

'Quite a bit of this could probably be verified by the chap at Grey's Garage,' the latter said thoughtfully. 'The vital bit is the interval between Forbes leaving for Durnycombe and passing Grey's again on his way back, isn't it? Was it long enough for him to get there, knock out Paterson, heave him into the Caravette and manoeuvre it over the edge? You'd better get along there early tomorrow morning and see the garage man before you go to the cliff area. Time yourself, and then go and see what progress the helicopter people and the coastguards are making. The only thing we can do now is to get Coryport cracking on tracing a possible trip by the Caravette on the road between them and Grey's that morning. It looks as though we could be in for more than we bargained for at the start, doesn't it?'

After a satisfactory conversation with the police superintendent at Coryport, Nevinson sat on at his desk for a brief interval, indulging in a pipe dream of successfully handling a headline-hitting case as his friend Chief Superintendent Pollard so often seemed to do. Then, having a sense of humour as well as ambition, he grinned at himself and headed for home.

*　　　*　　　*

Virginia Nevinson had been to a domestic science college and was an expert cook. A delectable meal was followed by superb coffee served beside the sitting-room fire. Charles gave a sigh of contentment and slumped back in his chair.

'God, I needed that nosh,' he said. 'And not the faintest suggestion of curiosity about what the heck I've been doing all day: you were born to be a policeman's wife. Actually, now I'm my own man again I'd like to clear my mind by recapping. Can you bear it?'

'I'm simply consumed with curiosity,' she told him. 'Is it that van of some sort that went over the cliff at Durnycombe?'

'How come you know anything about it?' Charles demanded. 'Don't tell me there's a leak at the station?'

'No need,' Virginia replied, indicating the television set and the local evening paper.

'Great heavens, have they got on to it already?'

'Only the baldest of statements and some shots of coastal scenery. Do tell me why you people are so involved.'

'Because the said van – more accurately a Roamhome Caravette – is the property of one Dr John Paterson of the College who hasn't so far reported its loss. . . .'

As he filled in the details up to date and Virginia sat listening, he saw faint signs of tension in her face.

'You're finding all this a bit reminiscent, love,' he said. 'The whole business could still turn out a mare's nest, you know, with Paterson ringing up to say he'd met a pal and gone off with him on a trip across the Channel or somewhere.'

'All the same you've pretty well written off anything like this, haven't you?' she asked.

'Well, yes,' Nevinson admitted as their eyes met. 'To be honest we have. . . . What exactly's getting under

35

your skin?'

'Those cliffs and the awful drop down. I can't help thinking of Jim Winch at that window at Marleigh Manor. And then money could come into it, I suppose. . . . Look at Nigel . . .'

Charles mentally consigned the Marleigh case to perdition, together with Nigel Kerslake, a connection of Virginia's by marriage who had treated her abominably. With a swift movement he scooped her up out of her chair and returned to his own, sitting her on his knee.

'You took me for better or worse,' he said, 'which includes my unfortunately necessary and often perfectly bloody job. Any regrets?'

'You know there couldn't ever be,' she told him, burrowing her face against his coat, 'whatever sort of worse there was . . .'

Chapter Three

By 9 o'clock on the following morning several operations were in full swing at Durnycombe. A Royal Naval helicopter from Gatherfield was in process of winching up the wreckage of John Paterson's Caravette in order to hand it over to the police for expert examination. A couple of frogmen were searching the underwater area all around. A rescue team of roped coastguards was slowly making the precipitous descent of the cliff alongside the Durnycombe Fall, and a search of the coastline was being carried out by boat. Charles Nevinson was interviewing the proprietor of Grey's Garage and his son who worked with him.

Both men struck Nevinson as reliable, and they were in complete agreement about the events of the evening of Friday 20th October and the morning of the 21st. Just after 5 on the Friday evening a gentleman had come up driving very careful-like in a Jaguar with its windscreen shattered. They'd told him they'd have to get a replacement from Coryport and couldn't fix it much before 10 the next morning. He – Mr Forbes, his name was – asked if they could hire him a car to get back to Minstow. When they said they'd got an old Mini he asked to use the phone to call his uncle in Minstow who'd put him up the night before and to ask if he could have the bed again. Then he went off in the Mini which they'd rounded up and they'd got on to their suppliers in Coryport.

'So Harry went over for the replacement right away,' Jim Bull, the garage proprietor concluded, indicating his son.

'And did you manage to get the job done by the time Mr Forbes turned up the next morning?' Nevinson asked, leading up to the more vital part of his enquiries.

'That we did,' Jim Bull replied with some complacency, 'an' with time to spare. 'Twas just on twenty to ten when 'e drove up in the Mini, and proper pleased 'e was. An' while 'e was startin' to write us a cheque for the job and the 'ire of the Mini that there Caravette went past towards Coryport. Must've been the one belongin' to 'is uncle as went over Durnycombe cliff. A white 'un. Turrible thing to 'appen. Reckon the poor gentleman must've gone with it as 'e's never turned up.'

'Did you see it go past, too?' Nevinson asked Harry Bull.

'Yea, I seed 'un. Chap at the wheel raised his 'and to Mr Forbes who waved back. There didn't seem nothin' wrong with the Caravette nor yet with the driver.'

'Then Mr Forbes went off with his new windscreen, I suppose?' Nevinson suggested. 'Will his insurance company pay up?'

'Sure, an' 'e won't lose 'is no claims bonus. But 'e didn't go off on the Minstow road right away. When 'e'd got 'is receipt, 'e began to shift 'is things from the Mini to 'is Jaguar, and 'e found 'e'd got 'is Uncle's camera in place of 'is own, and there'd been a mix-up. So 'e went along to Durnycombe to change over.'

'Tiresome thing to happen' Nevinson commented, 'holding him up when he was in a hurry to get off after all the delay.'

'"Twouldn't take 'im long. Us saw 'un comin' back and 'e gave us a toot as 'e went by. Just gone the quarter after ten it 'ad. We'd brewed up a cuppa and I can call to mind takin' a look at the clock up on the wall there an' thinkin' as we oughter get crackin' on the next job.'

Deciding that he must try out for himself the time it took to drive from Grey's Garage to Durnycombe, Nevinson thanked the Bulls for their help, warned them that they might be called on to give evidence in court and drove off, glancing at his watch as he did so. As the rough track at the end of the Durnycombe lane began to widen out into the expanse of bracken and heather at the top of the cliffs he saw two parked cars and a curiously immobile small group of men gazing seawards. . . . They've found him, he thought, conscious of an indefinable physical sensation. He drew up, and made a note of the time. It had taken him just under eight minutes to drive to the spot. He walked towards the watchers, and against the drone of an invisible helicopter learnt that a man's body had been found about halfway down the cliff and a stretcher lowered, but that bringing it up was going to be the devil of a job and take some time. After further discussion Nevinson drove back to Grey's Garage, his car radio being out of order, and telephoned to Minstow for a police surgeon and an ambulance to be sent out. The return trip had taken slightly longer owing to being held up briefly on rejoining the main road. The call put through, it was a case of returning to the cliffs and awaiting developments.

After telling the coastguards the steps he had taken he sat down with his back against a rock and took out his notebook. He began to put together a timetable of the events of the morning of Saturday 21st October, basing it on the statements of Mark Forbes and the Bulls and his own record of the time taken to drive between the garage and Durnycombe. Between intervals of staring abstractedly out to sea he finally produced a version that satisfied him.

TIME	EVENT	STATEMENT BY	CONFIRMATION
'About 9.10'	Paterson leaves Loyes Cottage in Caravette and M. Forbes in Mini	Forbes	None
'Just on 9.40'	Forbes arrives at Grey's Garage	J. Bull	Tacit (H. Bull)
?9.45 a.m.	Forbes writing cheque. Caravette passes. Driver acknowledges him.	J. Bull	H. Bull
?9.58 a.m.	Forbes leaves in his Jaguar for Durnycombe to change over cameras	J. Bull	Tacit (H. Bull)
10.16 a.m. (approx)	Forbes passes Grey's Garage heading for Minstow	J. Bull	H. Bull

He sat considering it critically. . . . It took me approximately eight minutes each way between the cliffs here and Grey's Garage, he thought. The Caravette would probably have been a bit slower, so if Forbes is lying and Paterson came straight here after all, he'd arrive at about five to ten, roughly ten minutes before Forbes. But if one can rely on the Bulls' timing Forbes was passing the garage again at eighteen minutes after he'd left it for Durnycombe. Allowing sixteen minutes for coming and going; he could hardly have knocked out Paterson and

40

manoeuvred the Caravette over the edge in two minutes. It would have needed at least five: he'd have had to get a conversation going to be able to take Paterson unawares, for one thing. Of course the Bulls' timing might be a couple of minutes out here and there, but they gave the impression of being dependable. . . . Obviously a charge of homicide based solely on this sort of timing evidence would never get past the DPP and into court, however convincing a financial motive there was. . . .

His train of thought was interrupted by the sudden revving up of the helicopter's engines, and he joined the coastguards as they watched it head out to sea, turn and make for its base at Gatherfield.

'Made our job a lot easier, these contraptions has,' one of the older men conceded.

As he spoke the sound of a motor vehicle coming down the track from the main road directed their attention inland. A car followed by an ambulance was jolting slowly over the rough surface. As Nevinson went forward both came to a halt. Three people got out, Dr Manningford, a police surgeon from Minstow, and two ambulance men. They paused to look at the retreating helicopter.

'I take it you've located what's left of the bloke on the way down?' Dr Manningford asked. 'Thrown out, I suppose?'

'About halfway between here and the bottom,' Nevinson told him. 'A stretcher's been lowered, but it's being a job to get it up as you can imagine.'

'Any idea when it happened?'

'Nothing definite. It could have been as long ago as last Saturday morning.'

Dr Manningford glanced at him speculatively. A faint shout, difficult to locate, seemed to come out of the air, and the coastguards advancing perilously near the cliff edge lowered further lengths of rope. A couple of minutes later as they heaved with all their strength the poles of a stretcher appeared, and finally the stretcher itself, with its lashed burden roughly swathed in polythene, was hoisted up by two exhausted members of the rescue squad. The men on the cliff top took over and carried it on to the level ground close to the parked cars.

In response to a nod by Dr Manningford the polythene wrapping was removed. One of the coastguards beat a hasty retreat and distressing sounds came from behind a clump of brambles.

'Front and right side of skull smashed in, left shoulder and arm fractured, left femur fractured', Dr Manningford remarked conversationally after a cursory examination. 'If you found him on the cliff face how come the external symptoms of either death by drowning or prolonged post-mortem submergence in water?'

One of the rescue squad explained that about halfway down the Durnycombe Fall a slight change of slope caused a pool to form before the water started downwards again. The body had been lying face down in the pool.

Expressing a hope that he himself would not be called on to pronounce on the actual cause of death, Dr Manningford instructed the ambulance crew to take the body to the mortuary at Minstow Hospital pending further instructions from the police.

'Hang on a minute,' Nevinson said. 'Do you recognise the chap?'

'Sure. John Paterson, a lecturer at Minstow College. A patient of mine, incidentally, and unusually sound in wind and limb. Over to you. I'd better push on and put the hospital in the picture.'

He drove off, followed by the ambulance. Nevinson waited behind to have a few words with the coastguards

42

and congratulate the rescue team on bringing off a difficult and dangerous job, and then headed for Grey's garage where he rang Superintendent Lock.

'What the hell can have happened?' the latter speculated. 'This looks like being a bloody time-consuming job for us. I'll get on to the coroner's office about the preliminary inquest, and then see Forbes. He's just got here. Get back as soon as you can make it.'

On arrival at Minstow police station Nevinson joined the two men in Superintendent Lock's office. As he shook hands with Mark Forbes he was reminded in a disconcerting if indefinable way of the face that had stared up unseeingly from the crumpled polythene on Durnycombe cliffs. . . . Paterson's greying hair must once have been this reddish colour . . . he pulled himself together and formally expressed sympathy.

'Thanks,' Mark Forbes said. 'It was you on the phone last night, wasn't it? I suppose I've been prepared for something like this since he presumably didn't show up, but it's difficult to take in, all the same. . . . What happens now? Do I have to identify him?'

'It isn't necessary unless you wish it,' Superintendent Lock told him. 'The police surgeon who was present when the body was brought up was Dr Manningford, your uncle's own doctor.'

He went on to explain the formality of the preliminary inquest, provisionally arranged for the following Monday.

'The coroner will take evidence of identity, issue a burial certificate and adjourn the inquest for enquiries to be made into the cause of the accident: possible mechanical defects in the Caravette, for instance and the state of Dr Paterson's health. We shall probably ask for an initial adjournment of a week. In the unfortunate circumstances you'll want to get into touch with his

43

solicitors, I expect? Do you know who acted for him?'

Mark Forbes passed the back of his right hand across his forehead.

'A Minstow firm. Bathurst and . . . and somebody. I've never met them.'

'Bathurst and Headley?' Superintendent Lock suggested.

'Yes, that's it.'

'Inspector Nevinson will have a call put through for you. Their office is only a few minutes' walk from here.'

'Thanks.' Mark Forbes sat frowning for a moment. 'If the inquest isn't till Monday, there's no need for me to hand around here, is there? I'd better go out and break the news to Mrs Dredge who was my uncle's housekeeper, and see the cottage is shut up and get the key from her, I suppose.'

'That's already been dealt with, Mr Forbes. An officer has been out and brought back the key which we must retain for the moment, I'm afraid, as a police enquiry into Dr Paterson's death is in progress. No, there's no need for you to be around over the weekend. We'll phone you at your home when we know the time of the inquest on Monday.'

Mark Forbes's head went up slightly but noticeably.

'Well, if I could contact the solicitors, then.'

When Nevinson returned from escorting Mark Forbes to the telephone and thereafter directing him to the office of Messrs Bathurst and Headley, he found that the Chief Constable had arrived and was discussing the situation with Superintendent Lock.

'My first reaction to this statement of Forbes about going in his car to Durnycombe and finding no sign of Paterson or the Caravette is that it's a shade fishy,' the CC said. 'You both heard it over the phone last night, I take it, and it was entirely unsolicited?'

'Entirely,' the Super replied. 'It came out apparently quite spontaneously in answer to a question of yours, didn't it, Nevinson?'

'Yes, sir. Mr Forbes stated that he had gone ahead of Dr Paterson on the Coryport road and was talking to the proprietor of Grey's Garage when the Caravette went past. I asked him if that was the last time he had seen his uncle and he said it was, and went on to explain that he then found he had Dr Paterson's camera and not his own, and drove over to Durnycombe to change the two over, but when he got there there was no sign of the Caravette or his uncle. He concluded that Dr Paterson must have found he'd forgotten something and gone straight to Coryport to replace it.'

'We've got enquiries under way about a white Caravette being seen on the road between Grey's Garage and Coryport from 9.50 onwards on the 21st,' the Super added, 'but nothing's come in so far.'

Major Waller looked up from the timetable put together by Nevinson.

'And those Bulls – father and son – strike you as reliable types who'd stand up to cross-examination?'

'Yes, sir, they do.'

'Well, add to that your own timing on the Grey's Garage to Durnycombe run, and I don't see how Forbes could possibly have pushed that Caravette over the edge in the time available unless he found Paterson sitting at the wheel already dead from a sudden heart attack, and if so, what would have been the point of it? Presumably the PM chaps will be able to find out if anything of the sort happened to Paterson.'

Nevinson repeated Dr Manningford's remark about John Paterson's state of health.

'H'm' the CC commented. 'Well, it's a case of waiting for reports from the backroom boys for the moment.

45

Unless you want to suggest any lines to follow up, Nevinson? You've been put on to the case by the Super.'

'Well, sir, perhaps we should get on to Mr Appleton as soon as possible. He may have information about Dr Paterson that might be relevant. Mr Appleton's due back from France on the Whiteharbour ferry this afternoon. We could have a message waiting asking him to ring us here on landing.'

Both the CC and the Super agreed that this was a sound suggestion, and Nevinson was told to deal with the port authorities and contact Paterson's solicitors.

'Dashed awkward for Appleton,' the CC remarked prosaically, 'losing a senior member of staff at the drop of a hat in the middle of a term.'

A call from Bill Appleton at Whiteharbour was switched through to Nevinson at 4.30.

'Appleton here,' came his voice. 'I've found a message asking me to ring you on landing.'

'Charles here, Bill. Sorry to meet you off the boat with this sort of thing but it seemed the obvious move to contact you at once. Briefly, Dr Paterson's met with a fatal accident. His Caravette went over the cliff at Durnycombe Fall.'

'*Paterson's!*' Bill Appleton's voice echoed the amazement of Mark Forbes on the previous evening. 'It's incredible! He knew those cliffs like the back of his hand. When did it happen?'

'We're not sure yet. Look here, it would be more satisfactory if you came along and saw me. Could you drop off Biddy with Virginia? She's expecting her, and there'll be a meal for you if wanted.'

'That's damn good of you both. We'll come straight on. God, what a thing to happen. Mercifully Grim-

46

shaw's used to coping with the routine side of the departments poor devil . . . We'll make it soon after 6 with luck.'

As he put down his receiver it struck Nevinson that Bill Appleton's reaction had been devoid of any expression of personal regret. Nor was there any sign of this when the latter turned up in due course, somewhat dishevelled in holiday clothes with his fair hair ruffled.

'Well, *de mortuis* and all that,' he replied when Nevinson asked about Paterson as a person. 'He was a sound middle-rank geologist with published work to his credit, and a good teacher, but as a human being, and a member of a community he was, in my opinion and that of a number of other people at the College, simply the bloody end.'

'In what way of ways?'

Bill Appleton gave a brief resumé of John Paterson's outlook on life, both personal and professional, including his treatment of Ronald Grimshaw.

'It was one of the best bits of news I've had since I became Principal when Paterson told me he had decided to accept the voluntary redundancy offer at fifty-five and push off at the end of this academic year,' he concluded.

Nevinson registered this relevant piece of information.

'I suppose you're filling in time before the reports come in from the PM and the mechanics?' Bill Appleton asked.

'That's roughly the position. Could his decision to retire at the end of the year be a pointer to suicide?' Nevinson said thoughtfully. 'I mean a diagnosis of cancer or something equally lethal? If so, his doctor knew nothing about it. He came out with the ambulance and made a remark about Paterson being unusually sound in wind and limb.'

47

'He might quite well have gone over his GP's head. Anyway you can rule out murder as far as College goes. Hardly worth it as he was going next July.'

'We'll have to come along to the College tomorrow sometime and ask a few questions though. On the suicide tack, about his state of mind recently, for instance. Who are the people who would have seen most of him?'

'His unfortunate second-in-command, Ronald Grimshaw.' Bill Appleton explained the organisation of the combined Geology and Geography Department. 'I don't know where Grimshaw's been this week. Then there's Paterson's secretary, a Mrs Brothers. We had a committee meeting on the morning of 20th October and he was present. I personally didn't notice anything unusual about him: he wasn't more than normally objectionable. I'll have to be around myself tomorrow trying to get hold of somebody to do his work temporarily, so ask for me if there's anything I can do.'

'Right. I will. Go along to our place now, and have something to eat. I'll join you as soon as I've got an appointment fixed up with whoever in Bathurst and Headley is Paterson's personal solicitor.'

After Bill Appleton had gone Nevinson sat on for some minutes reviewing their conversation. All very well to say that nobody at the College would have murdered Paterson as he was clearing out next summer, he thought, but there's such a thing as a last straw. . . . A last straw at Marleigh had produced murder, arson and ultimately suicide . . .

He decided that an interview with Ronald Grimshaw was fairly high on the priority list.

Chapter Four

Ralph Bathurst, the senior partner of Bathurst and Headley, turned out to be John Paterson's solicitor. He had been rather short on being contacted at his home on the previous evening, stating that he would be free from 9.30 to 10 o'clock, but not later on the next morning. Nevinson, aware of being little more than half his age, expected a difficult encounter and a cagey response to enquiries about his late client's affairs. In the event he was agreeably surprised. Bathurst was an experienced solicitor and looked the part, but made no attempt to hide his interest and curiosity.

'It's certainly an odd business,' he said. 'I suppose you people are checking up on side issues while waiting for the mechanics and medicos.'

'Exactly, sir,' Nevinson replied, 'And if both the *post mortem* and mechanics' report on the car are negative, if I can put it that way, we shall have to go into other possibilities.'

'Suicide or homicide, I take it?'

'Yes. So bearing these possibilities in mind we're naturally interested in who would benefit from Dr Paterson's death. Perhaps it would help matters if I tell you that Sergeant Andrews, who was sent out to Little

Underhill on Thursday evening to try to find out if anyone had any knowledge of Dr Paterson's whereabouts, questioned a Mrs Dredge, the daily woman at Loyes Cottage. She told him that Mr Mark Forbes had spent Friday night with his uncle, and added that when Dr Paterson died, Mr Forbes would 'get the lot' which was tied up on him by his grandfather's Will.'

Mr Bathurst sat in silence for a few moments, the fingers of his right hand tapping on the top of his desk.

'Under the circumstances,' he said at last, 'I feel I should give you the basic facts about Paterson's estate. He had a substantial income but the greater part of this was a life interest which under the terms of his father's Will reverts to Mark Forbes. He – Paterson – had been earning a quite hefty salary for some time, and although he did himself well, he wasn't a big spender and built up a nice bit of capital of his own. Every penny of this and all his chattels including the cottage at Little Underhill have been left to his old college at Cambridge.'

'Thank you,' Nevinson said, 'Has Forbes any other relatives who might conceivably contest the reversion of Mr Paterson senior's money?'

'None. Before you turned up just now I was looking through Paterson's file and came on this extract from his family tree which he gave me, with his Will and various other documents, when he took up his job here and asked me to act for him.'

Nevinson took the sheet of writing paper and studied it with interest.

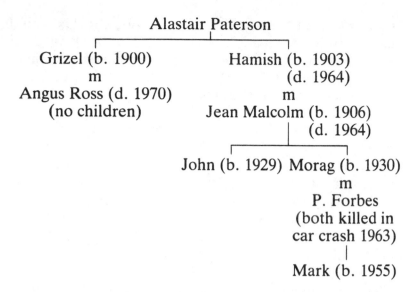

Alastair Paterson

Grizel (b. 1900)
m
Angus Ross (d. 1970)
(no children)

Hamish (b. 1903)
(d. 1964)
m
Jean Malcolm (b. 1906)
(d. 1964)

John (b. 1929) Morag (b. 1930)
m
P. Forbes
(both killed in
car crash 1963)

Mark (b. 1955)

'Grizel Ross,' Mr Bathurst told him, 'is a wealthy widow who has at the moment modelled her Will on her brother Hamish's. That is, John Paterson would have a life interest and the capital at his death reverts to Mark Forbes. I gathered from remarks of Paterson's that both prospective beneficiaries have been – shall we say judiciously – attentive to the old lady since her husband's death, but John Paterson on a number of occasions referred to her in anything but affectionate terms in conversation with me.'

Nevinson raised his eyebrows.

'Had you met Mark Forbes before he came to see you yesterday, sir?'

'No.' Mr Bathurst looked at him quizzically. 'This is a correct and tactful enquiry about my reactions, I assume? I expect you know that he's in Iremonger Properties. He's working his way up in that highly successful concern. I formed the impression – only an impression, I emphasise – that his sights are on a

51

partnership in the company, and no doubt this would involve putting in a tidy bit of capital. He struck me as an able and determined young man with an eye to the main chance. Incidentally, it came out in the course of conversation that his marriage has broken up. By his account his wife walked out on him a couple of months ago. His personal relationships seem to have been rather traumatic. As you see from that family tree he was orphaned at eight, and brought up in the family of his father's sister and her husband.'

'I'm awfully grateful to you for this filling in, sir,' Nevinson told him. 'Obviously there's a potential motive on the cards because of the terms of the grandfather's Will, but as of course you know well, it's means and opportunity that we go for in the first instance. But in confidence, although we're making a number of enquiries, results up to date have been entirely negative.'

Mr Bathurst made an indefinable sound in his throat suggesting understanding and speculative interest. Nevinson rose to bring the interview to an end and the two men parted on excellent terms.

Although Nevinson had laughed at himself for his brief vision of rising to fame through the successful solving of the Paterson case, he was determined to make a good job of his investigations. Mr Bathurst had asked for an unexpectedly early appointment. Grimshaw, who was next on the list, would almost certainly be closeted with Mr Appleton making temporary arrangements for the work of Paterson's students. It seemed good sense to let them get on with it for the moment and call at the Grimshaw home first. If the last straw hypothesis had any validity Grimshaw's activities on Saturday 21 October, would need close scrutiny. Admitting to himself that he might very well be wasting his time,

Nevinson drove from Bathurst and Headley's office to Rosemary Close, which was about ten minutes walk from the College. He drew up outside Number 3 and rang the front door bell of a modest mass-produced house. Within seconds there came the sound of footsteps running downstairs and the door was opened by a woman whom he placed in her late twenties. She had a sturdy little figure, curly light brown hair worn short and a clear complexion. Added to these assets were neatly cut features. Nevinson registered a small, rather tight mouth suggestive of determination and possibly obstinacy. She gave an overall impression of buoyancy. He presented his official card and was urged to come inside.

'I'm sure it's my husband you've come to see,' Linda Grimshaw said a little breathlessly, 'and I'm afraid he's out at the moment. Of course you know all about Dr Paterson's accident, and the Principal of the College has asked my husband to take over the Department at once. He'd have done so anyway next year when Dr Paterson was going to retire. Of course what's happened means there's an awful lot to arrange right away. Ron's over with Mr Appleton now, and I'm afraid I've no idea when he'll get back. You're most welcome to wait, of course. . . . Do let me get you a cup of coffee. I was just going to have one myself. You're lucky to catch me in, I'm on holiday at the moment.'

On impulse Nevinson accepted the offer. He spent the interval in assessing his surroundings. An adequate well-kept living-room, he thought, but very much first generation. Everything looked new. There was no sign of inherited family furniture or odds and ends, a minimum of photographs and no indication of personal taste in art. A curious assortment of reproductions of recognised masterpieces hung on the walls. The

Grimshaws are obviously on the social way up, he thought. Probably that was why Grimshaw had decided to stick it out as Paterson's deputy. A comparable job wouldn't be easy to come by at a time of reduced spending on education. And it was obvious that Mrs Grimshaw had social status ambitions. Over rather indifferent coffee he learnt that when her husband became Head of the Geography and Geology Department they would almost certainly move. The house was quite convenient, but not nearly large enough for the entertaining they would then be doing.

Nevinson manoeuvered the conversation round to the shock of Dr Paterson's fatal accident and thought he detected a hint of wariness in Linda Grimshaw's hazel eyes and about her mouth.

'I suppose you were both away at the time on your half term break?' he suggested.

'Actually we weren't for once,' she replied. 'I had been invited to help out at an old friend's wedding, and was away on my own from the Tuesday to the Sunday night. Ron wanted to get some work done so he let me have the car and was here on his own. We decided we'd just have days out when I got back. There's such a lot to discuss about our future plans, you see.'

She prattled on in the same vein. As soon as he decently could Nevinson extricated himself, saying that he would go to the College and see if it was possible to have a few words with her husband. He had at least collected two useful pieces of information. Grimshaw had been alone in the house on Saturday 21st October, the most probable date of Paterson's death. His wife could not possibly have been involved in it if she were away staying with friends, a matter which could be investigated if necessary. Her slight wariness at the mention of the fatal accident was, he thought, perfectly understandable. She must have realised from the start that the strained relations between Paterson and her husband were a matter of common knowledge and bound to come out, even if not already known to the police. He looked at his watch. It was nearly 11 o'clock, a reasonable hour at which to turn up at the College and ask to see Grimshaw.

He found that he was expected and a porter escorted him by way of the lift to Bill Appleton's office on the first floor where the latter was deep in discussion with a younger man looking harassed amid a litter of timetables and papers.

'Come along in, Inspector Nevinson,' Bill said. 'This is Mr Grimshaw, the Head of the Geography section of our combined Geography and Geology Department. Dr Paterson was senior to him and the overall Head, but Mr Grimshaw is taking over for the moment. Meanwhile we're trying to work out temporary arrangements for the students. We . . .'

He broke off to answer the telephone on his desk. Nevinson took the opportunity to size up Grimshaw. Middle thirties, he thought, and not particularly impressive. Mousey hair and unremarkable features apart from intelligent grey eyes. All the same, certainly not a weak face, although a sensitive one.

'Put him through,' Bill Appleton was saying. 'Possible temporary geologist,' he told Nevinson. 'Grimshaw, take the Inspector along and give him any help you can, and then get back here, will you? Sorry to push you off like this. . . . Yes, the Principal speaking . . .'

Nevinson was politely escorted from the room.

'The Department's on the next floor,' Grimshaw said. 'The lift's just along this corridor. We can use Dr Paterson's room if you like. Mine's a bit chaotic at the moment, I'm afraid.'

55

'I'm so sorry to have to bother you at this difficult moment,' Nevinson told him. 'I'll be as brief as possible.'

As they went through a door with a card in a metal slot inscribed DR J.H. PATERSON D.Sc. F.G.S. Head of Department' he was stuck at once by the pricey personal touches which its late occupant had introduced. Grimshaw pulled forward a couple of chairs and they sat down facing each other.

'Well, Mr Grimshaw,' Nevinson opened, 'of course you understand that it's one of the jobs of the police to investigate sudden deaths if there's no obvious explanation of what caused them. So far people who knew Dr Paterson find it quite incredible that careless driving on his part led to his Caravette going over the cliff. Apparently he was a very experienced driver and knew the area well. Would you agree?'

'Absolutely, Inspector.' Grimshaw leant back in his chair, crossed his legs and looked at him steadily, if impassively. 'He always knew exactly what he intended to do and did it, whether it was a matter of parking his car or ordering the affairs of the Department.'

'Right. Anyone can have a sudden lapse, of course, but at present we're prepared to accept the general estimate of him as a driver. Other obvious possible explanations of what happened are mechanical failure, or something like a sudden stroke or heart attack. At the moment the Caravette is being vetted by experts and a *post mortem* on the body's going on. But we can't disregard the possibility of suicide, and it's over this that I thought you might be able to help us. When did you last see Dr Paterson?'

'On the afternoon of the 20th just before the half-term break began. About a quarter to four.'

'Did you notice anything unusual about his state of mind, either then or earlier in the week, say?'

Grimshaw folded his arms and gave a short bitter laugh.

56

'None whatever. He had consistently been his normal perfectly bloody self. You've probably already talked to the Principal and know that Paterson has given me the hell of a life ever since I joined the Department. I've simply been a dogsbody and my geography students second-class citizens. There's no point in being reticent about it.'

'Leaving this personal relationship aside, what was his general standing with his colleagues?'

'People acknowledged his ability – as a geologist and a teacher – but I honestly don't know anybody who liked him personally. He certainly hadn't any close friends on the staff, and when he announced at the beginning of term that he was going to resign at the end of the year, the general reaction was thank God for that, anyway. You can picture mine, especially as the Principal invited me to apply for the headship of this Department in due course.'

'Were you surprised that Dr Paterson had decided to go?'

Grimshaw considered.

'Yes and no. He would have been fifty-five next summer and eligible for a voluntary redundancy cash handout which is quite generous. And he'd just had a book commissioned by a publisher. Not that money would have come into it all that much. It was well-known that he had a tidy private income and although he did himself quite well, he wasn't one to splash lolly about. No expensive girl-friend commitments, for instance. Anything in that line would be on a strictly business footing and well away from here.'

They sat in silence for a few moments while Nevinson turned over in his mind ways of bringing the conversation round to the weekend of Paterson's death.

'Oh, by the way,' he said suddenly, 'I forgot to say that

I went to your house before coming on here on the chance of finding you at home, and your wife was most hospitable. She insisted on my coming in for a cup of coffee, and happened to mention that you'd had work on hand over the weekend while she was on a visit to a friend's wedding, and this suggested another possibility to me. Did you by any chance work here late and hear Dr Paterson come back into College in the course of the evening, which, I imagine, would have been right out of character?'

Grimshaw, whose face had softened perceptibly at the mention of his wife, shook his head.

'It certainly would have been,' he agreed, 'but I'm positive he didn't turn up again before I went off myself about 5.'

'And he didn't ring you at home, by any chance?'

'Not unless it was after 7 when I went to some neighbours for supper. The Bidens, at Number 6. He didn't after I got back about 11.'

'We've reliable evidence,' Nevinson said, 'that Dr Paterson started off for Durnycombe at roughly 9 o'clock or a little later, on the Saturday morning, so if he tried to contact you before starting it would have been before then. You'll understand that why I'm harping on this possibility of his having tried to contact you or anyone else is on the chance of some evidence of mental disturbance. The suicide hypothesis, you see.'

'Well, I was out of my house by half-past eight that Saturday morning, so he could have rung me after I'd gone and before he started for Durnycombe, I suppose. Actually he very seldom rang me at my home. Probably he found it more satisfying to give me his orders by word of mouth.'

Nevinson decided against showing any interest in this very early start and got up to go. He stood for a moment taking a final look round the room.

'That second door,' he said, 'where does it lead to?'

To his astonishment he saw unmistakable shock appear and fade again in Grimshaw's face with the swiftness of a flash of lightning.

'Into the departmental secretary's office. A Mrs Brothers. We can go through to the corridor that way if you like.'

He followed into a small functional room in impeccable order, and without comment left it by a second door which was politely held open for him. As they went down in the lift he asked if he could have a word with any porters who might have been on duty during the late afternoon and evening of 20 October, and was led to a dapper grey-headed man in a cubicle in the main entrance hall.

'This is Inspector Nevinson, Holly,' Grimshaw told him, 'who's carrying out the police enquiry into Dr Paterson's accident. Give him any help you can, will you? And if you'll excuse me now, Inspector, I'd better be getting back to Mr Appleton.'

Holly, the College's head-porter, turned out to be an observant type with a sardonic streak. He had duly noted members of staff sloping off on the afternoon of 20 October before the official time of departure: half-past three. However none of these had belonged to the G. and G. as he called it. Mrs Brothers, the secretary, had left at close on ten to four, just after Mr Appleton himself. Dr Paterson had gone at just after five to four, but Mr Grimshaw must still have been upstairs at half-past four when Holly had handed over to Porter Barnett. By a stroke of luck Barnett was in the College. When run to earth he confirmed that he had unexpectedly found Mr Grimshaw still working in his room at about five minutes to five, but that he'd said he was just going, and had

59

cleared off by the time he –Barnett – had come back again after checking the upper floors. The main entrance to the College had been locked at five-thirty, and no one had rung for admission before Barnett was relieved by the night watchman at 9 o'clock.

At this point, Nevinson decided that nothing more was to be learnt from the College staff about John Paterson and his activities between his departure at just before 4 o'clock and the arrival of Mark Forbes at Little Underhill at about 6.30, according to his own statement. The dinner at the Crown could be checked but for the moment he allowed his mind to return to the most curious feature of the morning's interviews: Grimshaw's reaction to the apparently harmless question about the second door leading out of John Paterson's room. He asked Holly for Mrs Brothers' address and set off, ostensibly to question her about anything unusual in Paterson's behaviour during the past few weeks and gradually to lead up to the interview between him and Grimshaw shortly before the general dispersal for half-term. The most probable explanation of the latter's disquiet at the mention of the connecting door into her office was surely the sudden realisation that part, at least, of a significant conversation might have been overheard by Brothers.

For the first time that morning, however, Nevinson's programme failed to go according to plan. He rang the bell of the Brothers' flat and a woman emerged from the adjoining front door who told him that Mr and Mrs Brothers were away and not returning until Sunday evening. She eyed him with speculative interest and asked if he would like to leave a message with her. He thanked her but declined, saying that he would ring, and managed to extricate himself.

A more important setback was awaiting him at the

60

police station. Superintendent Lock glanced up as he came and tossed a report across his desk.

'Read that,' he said. 'One of our nice straightforward escape routes from this Paterson business gone west.'

The document was a detailed report from the team of engineers who had carried out the official examination of the wrecked Caravette. It stated categorically that there was no sign of any mechanical defect which would account for the accident. It also stated that when the vehicle had gone over the cliffs the handbrake had been off and the gears in neutral.

Nevinson grimaced as he returned the paper.

'At least there's the PM report to come in,' he said. 'The suicide possibility still stands.'

'It looks to me that for all practical purposes that report's in already,' the Super replied gloomily. 'Manningford's been on the line. He and the other two police surgeons are one hundred per cent definite that Paterson didn't have a sudden stroke or heart attack at the moment he arrived on the cliffs. There's conclusive evidence that he was dead before being flung into the water and they aren't satisfied about how some of the head injuries were caused, and have asked for a Home Office pathologist to come and vet them. Can't you picture the medical experts in court if we ever get as far as that? . . . Anything to report on whatever you've been doing this morning?'

Nevinson gave him the gist of his interviews with Mr Bathurst, Linda Grimshaw, her husband and the College porters. Superintendent Lock listened without interruption and was silent for some moments.

'Like Forbes,' he said at last, 'Grimshaw had a motive for liquidating Paterson, but a much weaker one. He knew that the end of the tunnel was coming next summer, whereas Forbes was faced with the fact that a hale and hearty bloke like his uncle could last on into his eighties or longer. But according to your reckoning, Forbes simply hadn't the time to do the job. . . . Picture those Bulls in court. There's nothing as immovable as a British working man if he's sure of his ground. . . . On another tack, what's your general impression of Grimshaw?'

'He grew on me, rather,' Nevinson replied thoughtfully. 'When I saw him first in Appleton's office he struck me as not having much personality and being in a complete flap over all the departmental problems that he'd suddenly been landed with. As if he'd got what he'd always wanted only to find that he couldn't cope with it. But when we went off together and got down to talking, I saw that he was an intelligent bloke capable of strong feelings – especially anti-Paterson feelings –even if not very forceful. He didn't seem in the least rattled by my questions until there was that sudden rather odd reaction to the one about the connecting door into the secretary's office.'

'On reflection what do you make of it?'

'I think it's possible that the interview between Paterson and Grimshaw that Friday afternoon was a pretty acrimonious one, and that Grimshaw suddenly realised that the secretary may have heard remarks that he'd made which he'd prefer not to come out in a police enquiry into Paterson's death.'

'H'm,' Superintendent Lock commented. 'You've probably got something there. Better tackle the Brothers woman first, and test the door as a sound barrier. Appleton won't like it, but that can't be helped. But as Brothers won't be available until Monday morning, you'd better lay off until you've seen her. You're supposed to be off duty tomorrow, aren't you?'

Nevinson replied that he was, but that staying on his

home ground was no problem.

'The preliminary inquest's been fixed for 11.30 on Monday morning to give Forbes time to get here. Make it clear to Appleton that you've got to see Brothers more or less as soon as she clocks in, however inconvenient it is. And when you go off duty this evening put the whole bloody case out of your head for twenty-four hours and come back fresh to it. It's a rum business, and I've got a hunch that we've barely scratched the surface so far.'

Chapter Five

Nevinson always maintained that the best thing about a day off spent at home was that life suddenly reverted to normal dimensions. Instead of incursions into previously unknown places to extract information from unwilling strangers, there were the restfully familiar surroundings and the shared interests and plans for the future. If the day off happened to be a Sunday, so much the better. Sunday had a particularly cosy and insulating feel.

This Sunday was wet, but no matter. Roland's playpen was installed in the sitting-room and while Charles and Virginia sat by the fire over some elevenses he astounded them by heaving himself up on to his feet and circumnavigating it from inside, grasping the rail for support. Progress was intermittent with frequent relapses on to his bottom but renewed each time with determination. The circuit completed Virginia snatched him up and cuddled him.

'Clever, clever boy,' she said. 'He's never been all round before, Charles, and he won't be one until Saturday. Don't you think it's wonderfully forward for his age?'

'He hasn't *said* anything yet,' the proud father objected teasingly. 'Only made animal noises.'

'Dad – Dad,' Roland enunciated, loudly and clearly from his mother's knee.

'And why not Mum – mum for heaven's sake?' Virginia demanded. 'Who bathes and dresses him, changes him, spoons his food into his mouth, pushes him out in his pram and whatever? The injustice of it! Here, take him while I prepare his dinner. That 'Dad – dad' should be his first word!'

She hugged him and handed him over to his father.

'Quite right, old fellow,' Charles told him. 'We chaps must hang together. I've seen more of life than you have. On Saturday you'll be one and I'll be thirty-seven.'

Roland was unresponsive. Experience had taught him that clinking sounds from the kitchen heralded food. He squirmed round to watch expectantly for his mother to come and fetch him, hungry after his exertions in the play pen.

Later, when he had been fed and settled in his cot for his midday sleep, Charles and Virginia had a leisurely Sunday lunch and returned to the sitting-room for a lazy afternoon, reading the papers in a desultory fashion, watching a short film on television and reviewing the arrangements for celebrating the joint birthday now less than a week ahead. Invitation cards to the tea party for under twos and their mothers had specified a duration of from 4.00 – 5.30 p.m. The daily would arrive as the guests departed and tackle the clearing-up while Virginia got Roland ready for bed. At 6 the trusted babysitter would take over.

'The relief will be marvellous,' she said. 'Just think of it: bathing, dressing up in my best kit and setting off for *your* party at the Crown without a care in the world.'

Charles wondered if she really had got over her hang-up over the Marleigh case. As if echoing his sudden unease the telephone rang. He went to answer it, fully expecting a summons to the police station, but to

65

his relief it was Bridget Appleton for a natter with Virginia. They had found everything OK on arriving home at their house in Marleigh, and Bill had managed to get hold of a quite reasonable temporary geologist. The conversation moved on to affairs in Marleigh where Virginia was still in touch with numerous friends, and ended with an undertaking by Bridget to look in at midweek when she came to Minstow to do some shopping.

'Bill wants just a word with Charles,' she concluded.

'Any developments, old man?' Bill Appleton asked.

'Only negative ones,' Charles told him. 'The inquest will be opened and adjourned at 11.30 tomorrow. We're asking for a week's adjournment.'

'Keep in touch if you can, and I'll do the same. We're both in for a pretty bloody week from the look of things.'

Charles Nevinson concurred.

'What time do departmental secretaries clock in?' he asked.

'8.30. If you want Mrs Brothers they'll be haywire in that department to start off with.'

'Fair enough. I'll lay off till 9.30, but she's high on the list, of course.'

Bill Appleton swore picturesquely and they rang off.

At the police station on the following morning Nevinson learnt from Superintendent Lock that the Home Office pathologist, Dr Eustace Newbold, had arrived on Saturday night, and work on the *post mortem* had continued on Sunday.

'A top-notcher, I should say,' was the Super's verdict. 'He agreed with our people that the head injuries have got to be investigated damn thoroughly. Apparently underneath the superficial ones caused by Paterson

66

being flung out of the Caravette against the cliff face there are some others of a different sort, and which appear to have been caused earlier on.'

'Blunt instrument?' queried Nevinson.

'Could be. Anyway photographs have been taken which can be enormously magnified, and tissue samples for further analysis. Newbold wants the last word in scientific apparatus used on them and is taking them up to the Yard labs. So – '

He broke off to answer the telephone.

'Put him through,' he said. 'It's Appleton. He wants to speak to you urgently.'

Nevinson went over to the extension.

'Can you come round right away?' he heard. 'When I started on my mail just now I found a handwritten letter from Paterson dated Friday 20 October.'

'OK,' he replied aware of an undercurrent and tension in Bill's voice. 'I'll be right along.'

'What the bloody hell now?' demanded Superintendent Lock. On hearing of this new and unexpected development he groaned. 'Anyway, don't forget the inquest at half past eleven. It looks better if we both turn up.'

On arriving at Minstow College a quarter of an hour later Nevinson found Bill Appleton dictating to his secretary. Formally dressed in a dark suit and with hair sleeked down he was functioning in his official role of Principal of Minstow College, but Charles who knew him well immediately realised that something had seriously disturbed him. When the secretary had gone out Bill opened a drawer in his desk and took out two letters on identical sheets of official college writing paper with the official heading *Minstow College – Department of Geography and Geology*. Both were handwritten.

'Read these,' he said briefly, pushing them across the desk.

The first was a personal note:

Dear Appleton,
To avoid any possibility of misunderstanding I enclose a formal withdrawal of my resignation from the headship of this department as from the end of the current academic year.
Yours sincerely
John H. Paterson

The enclosure was formal:

Dear Principal,
You will recall that I told you informally at the end of the summer vacation that I intended to apply for voluntary redundancy at the end of the current academic year when I shall have reached the age of fifty-five. On thinking the matter over further I have changed my mind, and shall be staying on in my present post, probably until I reach the compulsory retirement age of sixty.
Yours sincerely
John H. Paterson

'How did these letters reach you?' Nevinson asked, handing them back.

'My secretary says that Mrs Brothers – that's Paterson's secretary – brought in an envelope containing them both just after I'd left on the afternoon of the 20th, and said his instructions were that it was to be given to me this morning when the second half of term started up. Needless to say, I haven't told her what's in them.'

'Thank the Lord there are a few people around with

some discretion. It's obviously vitally important that it doesn't leak out at the moment. Can you remember at all accurately what time it was when you went off?'

'Quarter to four, as near as no matter. Biddy was to arrive then with the car and the luggage to give me time to drop in on you and Virginia. I had a word with Holly, the head porter, and went out to the car park. Biddy had just turned up. While we were checking over our luggage Paterson came by and we exchanged a few remarks about holiday plans before we drove off. That was the last I saw of him. It must have been quite 4 o'clock by then. If you're still interested in his state of mind it appeared perfectly normal.'

'It becomes a side issue for the moment,' Nevinson said. 'The $64,000 question is now whether he'd just told Grimshaw that he was staying on after all. If he had, it alters the whole situation by providing Grimshaw with a credible motive for murdering him. Do you think it's at all likely that he'd been told?'

Bill Appleton sat frowning for several moments.

'On the whole, no,' he said at last. 'Paterson was always careful to keep on the right side of the law, so to speak. In this case it would have been recognised procedure to inform me first when making a final decision about retirement. On the other hand, as I've told you, he gave Grimshaw the hell of a life, exploiting him abominably. If on that Friday afternoon they had an outsize row, he mightn't have been able to resist the sadistic pleasure of telling Grimshaw that he'd decided to stay on.'

'Thereby providing Grimshaw with this theoretically credible motive for liquidating him,' Nevinson said thoughtfully. 'Do you know of anything that might have sparked off a major row?'

'I suppose,' Bill Appleton said with obvious

69

reluctance, 'I'd better tell you about the Grainger Award'.

Nevinson listened attentively.

'I'm not going off at a tangent,' he said, when the statement ended, 'but what's your opinion of Mrs Anne Brothers, the departmental secretary? Do you consider her a reliable person?'

'I hardly know her personally: I have very little contact with the departmental secretaries. She must be reliable and efficient at her job or Paterson wouldn't have kept her for a week. My impression of her is that she's a detached impassive type. Not much imagination. I should think you'd find it pretty easy to get information out of her. What do you want to know?'

'Anything she knows about the Paterson-Grimshaw interview. What it was about and when it started, and if it was still going on when she left to give that envelope to your secretary. When I asked Grimshaw almost casually about the door leading from Paterson's room into her office he looked scared stiff for a split second, as if he'd realised its possible significance for the first time. Holly says she – Brothers – went out of the building just after you did, so she must have left her own office quite by a quarter to four. And as a check on her, we'll want to test just how sound-proof the connecting door between Paterson's room and hers is.'

'God!' commented Bill Appleton with feeling. '*Crime at the College*. Go ahead, of course. Not that I've any power or wish to stop you. The sooner this business is cleared up, the better. Could I suggest that you bring or send some of your chaps along to keep that part of the corridor clear while you're seeing how much can be overheard between the two rooms? The prospect of increased press and media involvement's making my blood run cold.'

70

'Ours, too. We'll do that thing. And if I can see Mrs Brothers now I'll remove myself from the premises as soon as possible.'

He got up, his eyes meeting Bill's keen light-blue ones, intelligent and troubled.

'Naturally I know your job involves facts and not opinions, old chap,' the latter said, 'but I can't refrain from saying that I just don't see Grimshaw as a killer. No comment required. Holly will get Brothers for you and fix you up with a room.'

Nevinson raised a hand in a sympathetic gesture and departed, aware that he himself was not looking forward to the inevitable interrogation of Grimshaw.

As he went through the usual preamble of explaining the reasons for his presence and need of her help in the enquiry into Paterson's death, Nevinson decided that his impressions of Anne Brothers coincided quite closely with Bill Appleton's. They had been allotted a small and rather stuffy waiting room, and sat facing each other across a table on which an assortment of pamphlets about Minstow College and its activities was displayed. He registered a rather large flattish face and a close-cut hair style which in his opinion did not suit it. Definitely impassive, he thought, not to say detached and unconcerned with anything that's not strictly her business.

She listened to him attentively as if receiving instructions from an employer, and replied that she quite understood.

'Well, as I said, Mrs Brothers,' he resumed, 'we are naturally interested in everything Dr Paterson did during the afternoon of Friday 20 October, the day before he met his death. I expect you took in his letters

71

for him to sign in good time because of Mr Grimshaw's appointment?'

She replied with a hint of disapproval in her voice that Mr Grimshaw had not made an appointment. He had simply come to her office after she had taken in the letters at a quarter past three, and said he must see Dr Paterson on an urgent matter. She had tried to put him off, saying that Dr Paterson was in a hurry to get away, but he'd insisted on seeing him before the half-term break.

'Did he say what this urgent matter was?'

Anne Brothers hesitated slightly.

'No. Only that it couldn't wait until after half-term.'

'But you knew, didn't you?' Nevinson risked.

'Well, yes, I did, after I'd been in to Dr Paterson, when he'd rung to say his letters were ready, and I told him Mr Grimshaw was waiting to see him urgently. Dr Paterson said he supposed the result of the Grainger Award had leaked out, and that I was to tell Mr Grimshaw that he could only have five minutes.'

'Can you remember what time it was when Mr Grimshaw went in?'

'Nearly twenty to four. I'd got my eye on the time because of getting off myself.'

'I know what the Grainger Award is,' Nevinson told her, 'so you needn't bother to give me any details about it. But what I do want to know is whether by chance you overheard any of the conversation between Dr Paterson and Mr Grimshaw. I'm not suggesting for a moment that you deliberately listened in, of course, but after all there is a communicating door between the two rooms.'

Rather to his surprise Anne Brothers showed no sense of outrage at this enquiry.

'Well, yes, I couldn't help knowing that there was a well, not very friendly discussion going on, and that it was about a geology student having got the whole of the Grainger Award money for this year. It's often divided up. If people on the other side of the door raise their voices or laugh or cough, anybody in my office is bound to hear anyway some of what's being said.'

'Did you hear the end of the discussion?'

'No. As soon as I'd got Dr Paterson's letters ready for the post and entered them up in the stamp book I dashed off. I had to drop in an envelope on the Principal's secretary on the floor below, and my husband was bringing the car to pick me up at quarter to four. She – Miss Winter, Mr Appleton's secretary –said I'd only missed him by about a minute, but it didn't matter because Dr Paterson had said the letter was for after half-term.'

'And as you left your office the discussion between him and Mr Grimshaw was still going on?'

'Yes, but I was in such a hurry that I didn't take in what was being said. All I remember is Dr Paterson's voice saying something about a settlement pattern, whatever that is.'

Nevinson took her over the ground again, making brief notes as he did so, but she stuck doggedly to her original statements.

'We shall be asking you to read a written account of what you have been telling me, and to sign it if you agree that it's correct,' he told her.

'Yes,' she replied unemotionally. 'I'm here from 8.30 to 4.30 during the week. If that's all, could I go now? There's a lot to do in the department as things have turned out.'

Nevinson let her go, wondering irrelevantly what it would be like to be married to her. One thing was certain. In the witness box she would be unshakeable, and he was no nearer finding out if Paterson had told

73

Grimshaw about his staying on as head of the department. The blasted woman had cleared out just a few minutes before the row probably reached its climax – if Grimshaw was speaking the truth when he said he'd last seen Paterson at about ten minutes to four. Anyway, Paterson left at just after five to four himself according to that observant bloke Holly, so they couldn't have gone on slanging each other much longer. . . . Perhaps the time spent on Brothers hadn't been entirely wasted, though. Grimshaw's evidence could be checked against her baldly factual statements for the period they covered.

The inquest on John Paterson's death lasted barely ten minutes. The coroner took evidence of identity, issued a burial certificate and granted the adjournment of a week requested by Superintendent Lock to enable further enquiries to be carried out. As the court dispersed, Mark Forbes, who had attended in the company of Mr Bathurst, came up to the police with a certain assurance in his manner. He explained that he had first to make arrangements for his uncle's funeral, but would call at the station during the afternoon.

'At Mr Bathurst's suggestion I'm asking Mr Appleton to join us for lunch,' he said, 'as obviously the College will want to be represented.'

Back in the Super's office Nevinson remarked that it would be more a case of having to be than wanting to be represented.

'At least that's one problem that's on somebody else's plate, thank the Lord,' Lock replied. 'Before we go off to get a spot of lunch ourselves, what's your next move going to be now that you've got the Brothers woman's statement?'

Before Nevinson could answer there was a buzz from the station's telephone switchboard operator. Lock picked up the receiver, listened, and frowned.

'Who the hell *is* this Mrs Grizel Ross of Lodwick, Northshire, who wants to speak to me personally?' he demanded, indicating the extension to Nevinson.

'She says she's the late Dr Paterson's aunt, sir, and has some information to give in connection with what she calls his murder, but she'll only give it to the head of the Minstow force. She rang half an hour ago while you were still at the inquest.'

'What does she sound like? The usual crank phoner-in?'

'She didn't give me that impression, sir. Elderly, but makes herself quite clear.'

'Better put her through, then, I suppose.'

During this conversation Nevinson had contrived to open his briefcase, get out the case file and extract the genealogical table of the Paterson family supplied by Mr Bathurst, and push it across the desk to Superintendent Lock as the latter was making himself known to Grizel Ross.

An elderly voice, crisp and decisive, came over the line.

'I must be brief, Superintendent,' it said. 'I do not want my companion Jean Naylor to overhear what I have to say. She is out shopping but may return at any moment. Regrettably you were out when I rang earlier. I have information which could help you to find the murderer of my nephew, Dr John Paterson. Obviously he was murdered. Please send one of your officers up here to see me as soon as possible.'

Lock grimaced at Nevinson.

'I'm afraid we're very short-handed at the moment, Mrs Ross,' he replied. 'It would be difficult for me to spare a senior officer just now. Could you perhaps let me have your information in writing?'

'I have no intention of putting the information I have to offer you on paper, Superintendent,' the voice informed him with acerbity. 'If you are unwilling to be co-operative I shall contact Scotland – *Good*bye, so *very* kind of you to ring,' the speaker concluded in a different tone and the click of a replaced receiver was audible.

The two men looked at each other.

'Well, what the hell do we make of that?' Lock asked. 'Write the old girl off as one of those who'll do anything to get some notice taken of 'em? Or do we contact the police HQ of her area and get the lowdown on her. Can't say I fancy the Yard being dragged into it, although God knows it may come to that.'

Nevinson sat ruffling up his dark hair for a few moments and finally came down in favour of the alternative course of action. He pointed out that if the PM report confirmed that Paterson had been killed by a bash on the head before the Caravette went over the side, and if Grimshaw could produce a watertight alibi for 21 October, they were without a single lead. He offered to do the telephoning himself. The Northshire police were co-operative, and undertook to ring Minstow back as soon as they had done some checking up.

Ten minutes later he was letting himself in at his front door, and was greeted by an unusual spicy smell emanating from the kitchen. Virginia was bending over a large fruit cake in the act of withdrawing a testing skewer.

'Done to a turn,' she said, inspecting the result. 'Your birthday cake for Saturday. Stage One.'

'Have you managed to produce any lunch as well?' he asked, kissing the top of her head. 'I'm ravenous.'

She gave him a swift questioning look.

'Yes,' he told her. 'Just the sniff of an unexpected lead.'

Chapter Six

The report on the *post-mortem* on John Paterson arrived
at Minstow police station in the early afternoon. The
forensic experts at Scotland Yard confirmed the
suspicions of the Home Office pathologist and Dr
Manningford and his colleagues that the dead man's
injuries fell into two distinct categories. Investigations
of photographs and tissue samples established beyond
doubt that the cause of death had been a violent blow on
the skull in the right parietal region. This had been
inflicted before a number of subsequent surface injuries
were sustained, all of which were consistent with the
body having been in contact with an uneven rocky
surface in the course of being flung out of a vehicle
falling headlong down the face of a cliff. It had finally
come to rest face downward in fairly shallow water.
Owing to the lapse of time between death and the
discovery of the body it was impossible to be precise
about the interval between the two types of injury
sustained or the time of death, but the experts were of
the opinion that it was not less than two hours.

Superintendent Lock took the report back from
Nevinson, read it for the second time and tossed it on to
his desk.

'Well,' he said, 'here we are landed with a deliberate cold-blooded murder on our plate and so far damn all to go on. Counsel for the defence would make mincemeat of the timing of that first injury. Nobody has come forward and reported seeing a white Caravette on the Minstow-Coryport road any time after 10 on that Saturday morning. There's nothing in any of these.' He indicated a small heap of reports from sub-stations in the area. 'No gangs of toughs around that morning and no homicidal maniac reported missing from a loony bin. As you said earlier, Grimshaw's alibi's our only remaining lead to work on, and as we've no possible means of establishing that he knew Paterson was withdrawing his resignation, I don't see how a case could be made out against him. Unless a chap's insane, and Grimshaw obviously isn't, one must be able to suggest a motive for a planned murder like Paterson's. When are you going to interview Grimshaw again?'

'I think,' Nevinson said, after consideration, 'that it would pay off to wait until tomorrow. He'll have had the hell of a day today trying to get the department functioning, and he'll only be unco-operative if I dig him out and start pressing him about where he was and what he was doing from 8 o'clock onwards on Saturday 21 October.'

Lock gave an assenting grunt.

'Then, I suppose,' he said, 'always assuming he'll be co-operative, it'll be a case of tracking down witnesses to get confirmation. God only knows where the manpower's coming from,' he said gloomily and fell silent, aware of the obvious solution that one way out of the dilemma would be putting it to the CC that the Yard might be asked to take over the Paterson case, and also that he himself would be extremely reluctant to make this move. He had a high opinion of Charles Nevinson's

78

ability and a genuine personal liking for him. Sheer force of circumstances had made bringing in the Yard on the Marleigh case inevitable. It would be bloody hard luck on him if history repeated itself over the Paterson affair. . . . Lock shot a quick glance at Nevinson and wondered if the possibility had occurred to him. Almost certainly, he thought.

A buzz from the internal telephone switchboard operator cut in on the silence that had fallen. Lock picked up the receiver, and a moment later gestured towards the extension.

'Yours,' he said. 'Northshire County Police. About Ross, presumably.'

Nevinson found himself in conversation with a Chief Inspector Tribe. Mrs Grizel Ross, he learnt, was the elderly childless widow of a well-known local solicitor. She was well-heeled, and although now over eighty years of age and living quietly at her home in Lodwick, she had formerly taken an active part in the life of the area as a JP, a school governor, chairman of the local Conservative party and so on. A very capable and energetic lady, in fact.

'Just a minute,' Nevinson cut in. 'The reason why we've rung you people for information will have been passed on to you: her claim to have information relating to the death of her nephew, the late Dr John Paterson, under suspicious circumstances near here. What about her mental state these days?'

Inspector Tribe assured him that mentally Mrs Ross was perfectly sound.

'She had a damn good letter in the Northshire News only last week about the state of the roads round Lodwick,' he said. 'A determined old lady, I'll grant you, but there's nothing of the crank about her.'

Nevinson asked if in recent years there had been any trouble at Mrs Ross's house reported to the police.

'Nothing of that sort,' Inspector Tribe replied. 'She's not one of those who ring up about noises in the night and whatever. Our chap who's responsible for the Lodwick area has been there six years and she's never called him in.'

'Does she have many visitors?'

'Not many these days our chap says. There's a great-nephew who works for some big London property concern who turns up for a night or two every few months, and this Dr Paterson you're interested in has come now and again. That's about the length of it.'

Nevinson thanked him appreciatively for so quick and full a response to the Minstow SOS, and was assured of any further help needed. He rang off. There was a lengthy pause during which Superintendent Lock sat with his left elbow on his desk, resting his chin on his left hand and staring in front of him with narrowed grey eyes.

'If you lay off questioning Grimshaw till tomorrow morning, and I agree it's a sound idea, it leaves the afternoon and Wednesday for getting the checking of his alibi going and briefing Andrews to take over. By making an early start on Thursday you could get up to Northshire in plenty of time to see Mrs Ross that evening and take a statement from her. Make sure the nurse hasn't got her ear glued to the keyhole by the way. Sounds a snooper. Then you get back here Friday afternoon. What about that?'

Suddenly and unexpectedly hopeful, Nevinson looked at him in surprise.

'You feel it's worth the trip, Super, even though she's eighty-three and can't get around much?'

'Don't forget what Bathurst said about the old girl's money being at her own disposal, and Paterson and Mark Forbes being attentive, with an eye to the main

80

chance, of course. According to the Northshire police she's no fool, and may have picked up some useful information about Paterson in particular. And about the trip being worth it, go back to what we were saying before Northshire called us. Even if we can bust Grimshaw's alibi we're still up against the question of motive. As I see it we can't afford to miss out on any lead at the moment. I took the incoming call from the old girl, so I'll ring her back right now and tell her that one of my most senior officers will call on her Thursday afternoon. That ought to keep her quiet and stop her trying to bring in the Yard. . . . Forbes is taking the hell of a time over his lunch, isn't he? My guess is that he's gone back with Bathurst to the office and is trying to find out what's coming to him in hard cash now Paterson's out of the way.'

It was nearly 4 o'clock when Mark Forbes eventually appeared. There had been a good deal of business to discuss, he explained, in connection with the reversion of his uncle's life interest in the Paterson family money to himself. Nevinson noted a certain sleekness about him as he talked, tinged with a degree of anxiety over the length of time enquiries into the exact circumstances of John Paterson's death were likely to take.

Superintendent Lock came bluntly to the point.

'I'm sorry to have to tell you, Mr Forbes,' he said, 'that the *post-mortem* examination has established beyond any doubt that Dr Paterson was murdered. His death was due to a violent blow on the head which he received at least two hours, according to the experts, before the Caravette went over the cliff.'

The sleekness was abruptly wiped off Mark Forbes's face. He stared at Lock with an expression of utter incredulity and amazement, his mouth slightly open.

'But who on earth . . . it's simply fantastic . . . I don't

believe they can be as sure of the time as that. I suppose some drop-out must have been hanging about on the cliffs when he got there and demanded money. . . . Uncle John would have put up a fight: he was that sort. But if he was trapped in the Caravette, of course . . .'

'If your reconstruction's correct, Mr Forbes, whoever attacked Dr Paterson didn't rob him. His wallet, cheque book, credit card, spectacles and valuable watch were all found on his body. Everything he had on him and with him is here in our custody.'

'Obviously the bastard must have panicked when he saw he'd killed Uncle John, and decided that the best thing to do was to make it look like an accident and shoved the Caravette over the edge. . . . You people practically always get thugs like this in the end, don't you?'

'Frequently, let's say,' Superintendent Lock replied. 'We've lost a little time following up the possibility of unsuspected mental illness and suicide, but now a full-scale murder investigation is on. You may be able to help us. Dr Paterson doesn't seem to have been what one would call a sociable type. Of course in his position he had a good many local acquaintances but apparently no close friends. Do you know of any non-local ones, or of anyone he had ever had a serious quarrel with?'

Mark Forbes rested his elbows on his knees and pressed the palms of his hands against his forehead.

'The truth is,' he said, resuming a normal position after a few moments, 'that I've never seen much of my late Uncle. My parents were killed in a car crash when I was eight, and I was brought up by my father's sister and her husband. Apparently Uncle John refused to be involved in any way and I hardly ever saw him. When I grew up and the terms of my grandfather's Will were explained to me, I decided to try and establish at any

82

rate a minimal contact with him. Damn it all, he was enjoying a life interest on the family money and had a good job into the bargain, and I could see that if I was ever going to get anywhere with Iremonger's I'd need some capital to put into the firm. However, although we got to a point at which he rather unenthusiastically put me up for the night when the firm sent me down to these parts to view properties, he clammed up if I started talking about my personal affairs. And he'd never come to my place when he was in Town at a geologists' conference or whatever. I never knew where he put up or anything about his private life except that he climbed in the Alps in the summer vacs. He was, to be blunt, utterly self-centred and contemptuous of his colleagues, especially his junior in the department. He asked me to call in at this chap's house one Saturday with a bloody rude message – an order, really, which I toned down. Mr Bathurst would bear me out about how little we saw of each other.'

'Of course we've had the possibility that Dr Paterson was murdered in our minds from the start,' Nevinson said, coming into the conversation in response to an almost imperceptible glance from Lock. 'The fact that you found no sign of him or of the Caravette on the Durnycombe cliffs when you went to sort out the cameras makes your suggestion that he'd driven on to Coryport the obvious lead to follow up. But in spite of intensive enquiries we haven't yet found anyone claiming to have seen either Dr Paterson or the Caravette. There has been an exhaustive search of the cliff top which hasn't produced a trace of anyone hiding in the bushes and other ground cover. About midday a party of students walked along the coastal path from Coryport to Minstow and met no one.'

Mark Forbes sat staring in front of him with a set expression.

'Is all this leading up to charging me with having killed him and sent the Caravette over the cliff myself?' he suddenly burst out. 'I'd got a motive all right, hadn't I? I've told you. Money.'

'Motive comes well down the list in a murder investigation, Mr Forbes,' Superintendent Lock told him, 'and opportunity right on top. And that's what you didn't have. We've carried out meticulously timed car runs between Grey's Garage and the edge of the cliff where the Caravette went over, and you couldn't have done it in the time you took on the trip to sort out the cameras.'

'Well, it's a relief to hear that from the horse's mouth,' Mark Forbes said, relaxing visibly. 'I don't mind admitting it. Ever since you people first rang me I've had the sensation of being caught up in a nightmare. . . . Have you anything else to go on at the moment? But I suppose one mustn't ask the police questions.'

'I can only say that we are taking all possible steps to trace other contacts of Dr Paterson's, both past and present. Inspector Nevinson will be going up to Lodwick shortly to see if Mrs Ross knows of any friends in your uncle's past. We'll be in touch with you, of course, Mr Forbes.'

When Nevinson returned from escorting out Mark Forbes the Super glanced up interrogatively.

'Any comments?' he asked.

'My impression was that he had been genuinely rattled because of the obvious money motive and being more or less on the spot at the time, and was very relieved when you told him he was in the clear. One thing struck me as a bit off-key, possibly. I mean Paterson's life outside Minstow and his job being such a closed book. Would it be worth asking the Yard if they can dig up anything?'

84

'Get a friend at Court on to it, in fact?' Lock suggested with a grin.

'The standard official approach,' Nevinson replied firmly, being sensitive on the subject of his personal friendship with Detective-Chief Superintendent Tom Pollard.

'Go ahead and make it, then,' riposted Superintendent Lock.

Nevinson gave a lot of thought to his forthcoming interview with Ronald Grimshaw. The case against him depended to a very considerable extent on whether he knew that Paterson was withdrawing his resignation. Mrs Brothers, the most promising source of information on this point, had turned out a dead duck. The main hope of finding out would be skilful interrogation of Grimshaw and the follow-up of his statements. Nevinson finally decided on a low-key approach, and to take along Sergeant Andrews to make a shorthand record of the conversation.

On arrival at the College on the following morning he was escorted to the Geology and Geography Department by a porter, and noted that the slotted card formerly on the outside of the door of John Paterson's room had been replaced by one inscribed R.F. GRIMSHAW M.A. F.R.G.S. On being ushered in he noticed some further changes. The two oil paintings, the handsome barometer and the bronze stag had disappeared. The desk at which Grimshaw was sitting was covered with papers of various types. He looked tired and strained as he got to his feet but there was an air of greater confidence about him. He's arrived, Nevinson thought, apologising for having to take up time at an inconvenient moment yet again.

85

'Of course you'll have seen it in the press or heard on the media that the *post-mortem* report is that Dr Paterson was murdered, and therefore his Caravette was subsequently sent over Durnycombe cliff with his dead body in it', he said, 'so a full-scale police investigation is now under way, and we are re-interviewing all his recent contacts in hopes of getting some information on what is a most puzzling case. I'll be as brief as I can as you've already been most helpful, but there are just one or two points I'd like to refer to.' He paused, and gave the impression of consulting his notebook. 'You didn't by any chance see Dr Paterson setting out on that Saturday morning? You both made early starts according the record, but yours was earlier. 8.30, according to my note of our conversation.'

He looked up to find Grimshaw eyeing him intently.

'I suppose you're thinking that anyone who gets cracking at that hour on a half-term Saturday must be either dotty or decidedly fishy. Here's the reason.' He opened a drawer and took out an aerial photograph. 'This first appeared in the *Minstow Gazette* a fortnight ago, and I went and got a copy from their office. Obviously it's the city in its natural setting. Do you notice anything in the north-west corner, high up on Twisterdown. Here's a magnifying glass.'

Nevinson decided to accept the gambit and scrutinised the area carefully.

'Very faint lines enclosing small pieces of land of different sizes and shapes. One or two darker and thicker lines. Possibly the bed of a small stream with shrubs alongside it,' he said after a pause.

'You could walk across it all and not see a damn thing except the channel of the stream. But the hot dry summer's shrivelled up the plant cover, and from the air the field pattern with enclosing banks and a couple of sunken lanes shows up distinctly. . . . In other words it's one of the 30,000 abandoned villages in this country, and there's no record of it. I'm a human geographer, and saw a chance of discovering another of these former settlements myself. So, as my wife was away, I decided to go off that Saturday with a camera and equipment and stake my claim to a modest discovery. Hence the early start.'

Nevinson had sufficient experience to recognise truth when he heard it. Grimshaw was obviously sold on early settlements. He decided to let him ride his hobby horse further before bringing him down to earth over the details of timing and the confirmation of his movements required for the record. He learned of twelfth-century land hunger and agricultural expansion into less fertile land with the accompanying building of villages. Then, in the middle of the fourteenth century the devastating tidal wave of the Black Death had swept over England, reducing the population of the entire country by something between a third and a half, inaugurating a withdrawal of settlement back once more to the more fertile lands which had continued well into the fifteenth century. . . .

'All this simply gets me hooked,' he said, 'and I do wish you luck with your further exploration of the site up there. Would that we could go on talking about it, but we're both pressed for time, worse luck. Could you just go over the route you took on leaving home, and try to remember anyone you met and roughly at what time? Like you over this abandoned village we try to build up a complete picture of a case by moving from one confirmed fact to the next.'

Grimshaw leant back in his chair and the tired and slightly strained look returned to his face.

'The trouble is,' he said, 'I met very few people and

hardly spoke to a soul all day. How well do you know this side of Minstow?'

'Pretty well. We're expected to know our way around. You started from your place in Rosemary Close, I take it?'

'That's right. I remember meeting our paper boy just as I came out into the road. Cecil Road, it's called, and I stopped at the little general shop to buy a slab of chocolate: Mowbray's Stores. Just beyond it there's a road on the right which is going to join Hill Road eventually, but it isn't properly made up yet. But you can get through on foot and I crossed Hill Road and –

'Just a minute,' Nevinson broke in. 'Was there much happening on Hill Road. Any car you specially noticed?'

Grimshaw shut his eyes and frowned. Finally he opened them again and sat staring straight in front of him.

'No,' he said, 'not much. I remember a lorry going in the Coryport direction just as I was coming up to the main road but the driver wouldn't have spotted me, I shouldn't think. Then I crossed the road and bore left, and a dark Mini went past in the other direction but I didn't pay much attention to it. And after about fifty yards I came to the lane leading to the farm on the lower slopes of Twisterdown and turned up it. There's a small farm a short distance up the lane but I didn't see anyone about. A dog ran out and barked a bit. I just pushed on. The lane soon became more of a grassy track and there's a small overgrown quarry about half a mile further on. I spent a bit of time poking about there, examining the rock face when I could get at it.'

'What were you hoping to find, as a matter of interest?' Nevinson asked.

'Evidence of early extraction of the stone. Sometimes you find fragments of a stone-built structure on these early sites, probably a rudimentary chapel if it's a moderately large and rather remote site. Anyway I found no convincing evidence of primitive quarrying, and think the stone which had been extracted was for the farmhouse I'd passed which had some sixteenth-century features. So I pushed on up Twisterdown and hit my target. It was quite a moment. I saw at once that I'd been dead right. The vegetation cover was so dried up that the boundaries of the small enclosures were perfectly clear. So were the low grassy mounds, almost certainly the collapsed rubble of peasants' houses, and one of these was much larger than the others, suggesting interesting possibilities. If only I wasn't so tied up with things here I'd have got the County Archaeological Society up there by now. I started in at once to make sketch plans and take some measurements and photographs, and after I'd been working for an hour or so on this the only people I met all day turned up: a man and his wife on a weekend walking tour. They'd been heading west along the coastal path and decided to come over Twisterdown and go down to Minstow.'

'Can you remember what time this was?' Nevinson asked.

'Quarter to twelve. The chap looked at his watch and said they'd easily make Minstow for lunch and then have a look round. I told them the best things to see and they pushed off.'

'You don't remember their name, I suppose?'

'We didn't get to the name-swapping stage. To be honest I was anxious for them to move on. They were interested in the site and asked sensible questions, but I'd only finished about half the plan I was trying to get done. Here it is, if you'd care to see it.'

'I expect it was late afternoon before you could tear yourself away,' Nevinson commented, after inspecting it with interest.

'I got home about half-past five with my sights on a hot bath and a decent meal in a pub. And if it's of any interest to you I ran into two near neighbours outside my house: a Mr and Mrs Best of Number 11 Rosemary Close.'

As they drove away from the College Nevinson turned to Sergeant Andrews.

'You're a local lad,' he said. 'How far would you say it is, roughly speaking, from Rosemary Close to this abandoned village site on Twisterdown?'

Andrews was silent for some moments while negotiating the exit from the College entrance into the main road.

'If it's where I take it to be, sir, I'd say six-and-a-half to seven miles.'

'Half-past eight to about a quarter to eleven, for, say six-and-three-quarter miles, including the stop in the quarry,' Nevinson commented. 'He certainly didn't belt along, but most of the way would be steep and pretty rough going, and I suppose he was looking around for possible signs of other former settlements.'

Back at the police station they pored over a town plan of Minstow and the relevant sheets of the two-and-a-half-inches to the mile Ordnance Survey map, using a small calibrated measuring gadget which gave the distance covered by Grimshaw as fractionally less than seven miles. Finally Nevinson sought out Super-intendent Lock who listened with interest but agreed that it was impossible to draw any definite conclusions from Grimshaw's statements.

'Of course, getting hold of that couple he says he met would be useful,' the Super said, 'but I don't see how it could be done without a broadcast and press appeal and that just isn't on at the moment. We haven't the beginnings of a case against Grimshaw as things stand –or anyone else for that matter. It's one bloody blank wall after another.'

Nevinson agreed.

'None of the chaps who questioned Paterson's colleagues at the College got anywhere. Well, if you still feel it's worthwhile my going up to Lodwick to see this Mrs Ross on Thursday, I'll make sure the case file's complete up to date and finish off any loose ends belonging to other jobs tomorrow.'

'You may as well go,' Superintendent Lock said with a marked lack of enthusiasm. 'At least it looks as though we're doing something, and there seems some evidence that the old girl isn't senile or plain bonkers.'

The Nevinsons' breakfast was normally at 8 o'clock. On Thursday morning Virginia, anxious for Charles to get off on the long drive to Northshire in good time, was busy cooking bacon and eggs by a quarter to eight. Roland had been bathed, dressed and installed in his high chair where he sat drumming on its tray with a spoon and eyeing his beaker of orange juice on the kitchen table. Suddenly there was a ring at the front door bell and a rattling of the letter box. Charles could be heard running downstairs.

'Got a birthday comin' up by the look of it,' the postman remarked.

'That's right,' Charles replied. 'Two, actually. My own, and my son's first. Next Saturday.'

'Be seein' you again I don't doubt, but all the best to both of you if I don't.'

The front door shut.

'One of the parcels is actually for me this time,' Charles called.

'You're not to open it,' Virginia called back. 'We'll

open them all at breakfast on Saturday. Anyway I've just dished up.'

'Just one peek at this book. It's been sent from Harridges. That'll be Aunt Lou, bless her, and the gardening book she knows I – '

For a split second the violence of the explosion paralysed thought, blotting out awareness of all else. A waft of acrid smoke came through the kitchen door. Virginia's world contracted to the dragging of Roland's chair to the back door and thrusting it outside. She briefly heard her own voice calling frantically for help but lost it as she tore to the sitting-room from which smoke was billowing out: Life became crawling on the floor so that you could breathe, grabbing the hearthrug and smothering and beating out the flames trying to envelop Charles's coat. Flying glass from the shattered window had cut his right cheek. . . . Someone else was helping her. . . . A voice in the hall was putting enormous urgency into the words 'fire brigade' and 'ambulance' and saying 'Vicars' Lodge' over and over again. And there was distant terrified screaming. . . . Roland's. . . . But all these things receded to infinity beside the fact that Charles lay perfectly still, his eyes closed. Only the thin thread of blood was moving slowly down his face.

PART TWO

Chapter Seven

As Detective Chief Superintendent Pollard of New Scotland Yard arrived in response to an urgent summons his Assistant Commissioner glanced up from his desk.

'That bloody place Minstow again,' he said while scrawling his signature to a document. 'You must have seen reports of a dormobile affair going over a cliff with a dead geologist in it. Apparently yesterday somebody sent the chap they'd put on the job a fairly potent letter bomb, and he's in hospital. . . . What's the matter with you?'

'Was the chap called Nevinson by any chance?'

The AC snatched up a paper, glanced at it and passed it over with others to Pollard.

'Charles Nevinson. Know him?'

'He was the chap I took over the Marleigh case from when they lost their Chief Super and a sergeant in a car crash on the ice. A promising type.'

'Well, your activities won't include going to his funeral. He was damn lucky, apparently. Just happened to have turned his head to speak to his wife in another room as he ripped open a jiffy bag. Superficial burns and cuts from flying glass and a dislocated shoulder. He was flung against some piece of furniture, apparently. The CC, a Major Waller, obviously thinks his men are going to be picked off one by one, and not unnaturally wants us to take over, and had the nerve to ask for you.'

'He was – is – Richard Bellamy's cousin, if you remember, sir.'

'Professional wire-puller, Bellamy, from the look of things. You'd better go down, Pollard. They seem to have done a reasonable amount of preliminary work on the case so with any luck you ought to be able to clear it up pretty quickly. You've got the advantage of knowing the set-up.'

'They've got a new Chief-Super since Marleigh,' Pollard pointed out.

'Don't quibble. And to save you the formality of asking permission you can take Toye.'

'Thank you, sir,' Pollard replied impassively, getting to his feet.

'Keep us informed. As usual you've hooked one of the interesting cases.'

As was his custom, Pollard spent the first part of the drive down to Minstow in the back of the Rover, digesting Major Waller's SOS to the Yard, and studying photostats of the file on the Paterson case and a selection from press coverage up to date. Eventually he put the various papers together and stowed them in a folder.

'Watminstow Service Station 4 miles,' he read aloud as a sign flashed past. 'Pull in for a quick if undrinkable coffee while I give you the gist of all this.'

Over the coffee Toye heard that the case had some rather unusual features.

'Deceased, Dr John Paterson, was a good second-grade geologist, was apparently universally disliked by his colleagues at Minstow College, and singularly friendless by choice in the world at large. His only surviving relatives are an aunt of eighty-three and a nephew of twenty-eight. The nephew to whom the appreciable family money reverts on Paterson's death is an obvious suspect who was around but has an apparently cast-iron alibi. The only other known suspect is a chap called Grimshaw who was the Number Two in the Geology Department and whose life was made unbearable by Paterson's bullying. His alibi is the negatively cast-iron type. I mean, he can't prove conclusively that he was where he says he was at the critical time, but it appears to be virtually impossible to prove that he wasn't, if you follow.'

Toye replied that he did.

'The aunt of eighty-three has rung up Super Lock and says she knows whodunnit, and would he please send up an officer at once. This was on Monday. Lock had the Northshire County Police contacted and they say she's perfectly *compos mentis* so Nevinson was to have gone yesterday and it looks highly probable that we shall be going instead, probably tomorrow.'

Toye, passionately addicted to cars and motoring, expressed his satisfaction at this prospect.

'The case might have been designed for you,' Pollard remarked. 'Finish your coffee and we'll push on. The first fence is going to be how Super Lock reacts to our arrival.'

The arrival in its first few moments looked as though it was going to be even dicier then Pollard had feared. Followed by Toye, he was ushered into a room occupied not only by Superintendent Lock but also by Major Waller, the Chief Constable of Downshire, with whom he had important contacts over the Marleigh case. Waller got up with outstretched hand and welcomed him

97

warmly before immediately introducing Superintendent Lock. Pollard shook hands with a tall man with a reddish tan whose brown hair was greying a little. He was aware of a swift appraising glance, and presented Toye to both the Minstow men. Waller looked at his watch.

'Unfortunately, I'm due at a meeting at Coryport in half an hour,' he said, 'but I know I'm speaking for Superintendent Lock as well as myself and everybody here when I say we're damn glad the Yard has sent you down with the special advantage of knowing the district. Nevinson's a valued and well-liked member of the Force here, and this vicious attack on him has got us on the raw. There's no proof whatever that it's connected with the Paterson case, but there's no one else gunning for him that we know of. Over to you, anyway. We'll let you have the report on the letter bomb as soon as the forensic chaps are through with it. I take it you were given the facts we sent up to the Yard with our SOS? Right, then. I'm on tap, of course, if I can help in any way. We've booked you in at the George and Dragon as before.'

As Toye closed the door after him, Superintendent Lock indicated a couple of comfortable chairs and rather tentatively suggested a drink.

'Could we not do with one before the mental filling-in starts?' Pollard responded with alacrity as Lock extracted bottles and glasses from a cupboard behind his desk. 'We're going to need the heck of a lot of help from you and your people, you know. Your CC's kidding himself if he thinks that knowing the local geography on the Marleigh side of Minstow's going to be much of an asset to us. As to the local inhabitants, I know Nevinson and his wife – I'm godfather to young Roland, actually –and I met the Appletons at Nevinson's wedding, but that's all it amounts to. . . . Cheers,' he added, as glasses were raised.

'I read up the Marleigh case with a good deal of interest when I first came,' Lock said, 'and thought young Nevinson got off to a pretty good start on it, but with that London red herring I reckon they'd have had to call in the Yard sooner or later.'

'Could be,' Pollard agreed. 'All the same it's rotten luck for him to have to hand over in midstream a second time. Look here, Super, what I suggest is that I just drop into the hospital for ten minutes, and then put in an hour on the case file with Toye at the George and Dragon before you join us for a meal if you can manage to. Then we can discuss the next move at leisure.'

Lock, who had clearly expected to be treated very differently by a Yard Ace accepted with alacrity.

Nevinson, in a private room at Minstow General Hospital, was positively enshrined in flowers, baskets of fruit, chocolates, Get Well cards, magazines and other tributes from well-wishers. His right shoulder and forearm and his neck were bandaged and plaster patches adorned his right cheek, but he looked surprisingly well and grinned broadly at Pollard.

'God!' Pollard remarked. 'It might be a film star's bedroom. A near shave though, old man. Oodunnit?'

'Oodun Paterson, possibly?' Nevinson queried. 'Up to you now, anyway. The Super says I'm good for at least a month's leave.'

'I had just to look in and see how much of you was left but I must push off. Lock's having supper with us at the G and D and we're planning the next step. If I don't let Toye drive me up to see Auntie Grizel he'll probably resign from the Force. You were going yesterday morning, weren't you?'

'Yea. I hope you'll go. It seems to me the only hopeful line at the moment. And could it possibly be that somebody didn't want me to make the trip?'

'If not, why not!' Pollard replied as he got up. 'Thereby might hang a tale. Love to Virginia and my godson. How is she?'

'OK. . . . Biddy Appleton has the situation in hand and isn't allowing her to be anything else. Decorators have been brought in already to repair the damage.'

Pollard gave him the V-sign as he departed and called in at the Ward Sister's office.

'Inspector Nevinson'll be scarred a bit,' she told him, 'but it's wonderful what plastic surgery can do these days. My word, what an escape he had! He might so easily have lost his sight. Shameful of whoever did it, and daft, too. I mean if you kill one policeman another pops up right away to carry on, so it doesn't get you anywhere.'

Pollard did not stay to debate this robust point of view but set off on foot for the George and Dragon, meditating as he walked. He was inclined to think that there was a connection between the letter bomb and the Paterson case, and that for some reason it had been vitally important for someone to incapacitate Nevinson. The sender must have thought that Nevinson either unconsciously possessed the clue to the identity of Paterson's murderer, or that he would discover it by visiting Grizel Ross. But any normally sane adult would realise that the police would quickly find a substitute for Nevinson. . . . Perhaps delay would enable evidence to be destroyed. . . .

At this point he arrived at the George and Dragon, and found Toye immersed in the contents of the file.

After an hour they agreed that Nevinson's handling of the case couldn't be faulted.

'The lot,' Pollard commented, stretching and clasping his hands behind his head. 'Genealogical table, timetables, map, statements checked and counterchecked. Unless either Forbes or Grimshaw or Mrs Brothers is an accomplished liar or somebody has been heavily bribed – the Bulls, for instance – it looks as though A.N. Other must be involved. And who the hell is he? Or she?'

They arrived in the reception area of the George and Dragon simultaneously with Superintendent Lock, and bore him off for a pre-supper drink. By common consent the case was dropped during the meal, the main subject of discussion being the relative advantages of static and peripatetic police work. When they had returned to the station and settled down in his office Lock asked Pollard if he had come to a decision about going up to Lodwick and interviewing Mrs Ross.

'Yes,' Pollard replied. 'Not that it looks a particularly hopeful lead, but because there doesn't seem to be any other obvious one at the moment. We'll make an early start, see her in the late afternoon or early evening, and get back as soon as possible the next day. Perhaps it's a bit late to ring the old lady tonight. Could it be done from here tomorrow morning?'

'I'll put through a call about 9.' Superintendent Lock made a note on his desk pad.

'At the moment,' Pollard said, 'the aspect of this Paterson affair that strikes us most forcibly is the importance of timing. For instance, the Bulls' statements about how long after Forbes's arrival the Caravette went past, and how long after that Forbes started for Durnycombe to change over the cameras, and finally drove past the garage again heading in the Minstow direction. All that business of looking at the garage clock while they were downing their cuppas. Then there's Mrs Dredge noticing the time when Forbes turned up at Loyes Cottage to deposit the camera. Is it all just a bit neat?'

101

'You'd expect the Bulls to have had an eye on the clock over getting the new windscreen fixed on time, and maybe having to catch up on other jobs,' Toye objected with his habitual caution.

'Fair enough,' Superintendent Lock agreed. 'But I reckon Mr Pollard's got his finger on something over this timing business.'

'On the same tack,' Pollard pursued, 'what about Grimshaw's alleged programme? Possibly just a few seconds before Paterson breaks it to him that he isn't clearing out after all, Mrs Brothers leaves her office. Or so she says. Is she covering for Grimshaw? Maybe she's speaking the truth, the whole truth, etc. Maybe Paterson never did tell Grimshaw. But it could make all the difference where a motive for Grimshaw to murder him is concerned. Then there's the definitely unsatisfactory timing of Grimshaw's activities on the morning of 21 October. Nothing between buying a bar of chocolate at roughly 8.40 and meeting up with a couple of walkers at this abandoned village place at a quarter to twelve. Distance to be covered just on seven miles. Did the couple really exist?'

Lock and Toye made noises in their throats indicative of agreement and mutual dissatisfaction.

After lengthy discussion it was decided to leave matters as they stood until Pollard and Toye returned from Lodwick with whatever information Grizel Ross produced. Unless some hitherto unknown person was involved, the odds were that she would produce some evidence against Grimshaw. It seemed hardly credible that she would deliberately expose her great-nephew to a capital charge, as according to Mr Bathurst she and John Paterson were far from being on affectionate aunt-and-nephew terms.

'Anything we can do in the way of making a few

102

enquiries on any other aspect of the case while you're away?' Lock asked.

'Perhaps you could carry on with an investigation into these various points, Super,' Pollard suggested. 'For instance, did anyone actually see the Caravette and the Mini going off together from Loyes Cottage at 9 or soon after that Saturday morning, and was Forbes seen by anyone leaving Little Underhill on the London road at about a quarter to eleven? It might be worth having another go at the people at the farm at the bottom of the Twisterdown Lane, and investigating the local reputation of the Bulls. And, of course, any trace of the alleged couple who turned up at the village site might be extremely valuable. Not asking much, are we?'

'Only too glad to dig something up if we can. Sergeant Andrews is good on ferreting out information without seeming to, if you get me,' Lock assured him. 'I think – '

He broke off as his desk telephone bleeped, listened for a moment and passed the receiver to Pollard.

'Letter bomb report,' he said.

Pollard listened attentively, occasionally cutting in with a question.

'Thanks a lot,' he said. 'Cherish the remains, won't you? It sounds a competent job at a rather elementary level,' he told Lock and Toye. 'Phosphorus, sugar and polythene bag geared to rip open when the opener strip of the jiffy bag's pulled. The typed label is partly one of Harridge's standard ones with the middle cut out and partly a blank insert with a typewritten address. Too scorched to detect any lettering defects.

After a few further points had been discussed the meeting broke up. Toye, who had marked down an all-night garage which satisfied his critical eye, took off the Rover for a tyre check and a fill-up with petrol against the early start on the following morning. Back at

103

the George and Dragon Pollard hesitated briefly and then dialled the Nevinsons' number. The ringing tone persisted and he regretted his impulse, picturing a small panic-stricken Virginia keyed up for an emergency call from Night Sister.

'Tom Pollard, my dear,' he said. 'I couldn't resist calling you to say I've seen Charles and think he's looking amazingly fit, and now I've obviously woken you up. So sorry.'

'Oh, Tom!' There was a little catch in her voice. 'It's been quite awful. If it hadn't been for Biddy and Bill Appleton I don't know what I should have done. Everyone's been marvellous.'

'Yourself included, I gather. Congratulations on becoming a fully blooded CID wife. Now listen. Toye and I are off at crack of dawn to follow up a lead, but we should be back on Sunday afternoon, tell Charles will you? You might even have got him home by then, from the look of him. How's my godson?'

'None the worse, as far as I can see. He yells "Bang!" with enormous enthusiasm about every five minutes. Come in as soon as you can, won't you?'

'Promise. Now return to your slumbers and bless you. My regards to the Appletons.'

It had been a long and wearing day. He relaxed in his comfortable bed letting his thoughts drift. Finally he fell asleep while reflecting that if the letter bomb was connected with the case, Grimshaw looked like having easier access to phosphorus than Forbes . . . labs . . . in . . . the . . . College.

The George and Dragon was situated in the mediaeval centre of Minstow. Toye, who invariably found the time and the means to do his homework before setting out,

104

negotiated the narrow streets with unhesitating confidence and took up his stance at the traffic lights which controlled egress on to the London road. At the first glint of green the Rover was away. Driving a car, particularly a top car conveying a Detective-Chief Superintendent of New Scotland Yard, was to him a continuous form of artistic expression, not a mechanical exercise. Not for the first time Pollard found himself enjoying the resolute assessment of opportunities and risks ahead. The early morning rush-hour traffic heading for Minstow melted away behind them as they headed for the motorway and the North.

As was often the case on a long run they would discover after a lengthy silence that their thoughts had been following the same track.

'Sounds as though the old lady's made up her mind and won't be easy to shift,' Toye remarked.

'This is it,' Pollard replied. 'We may very well feel the whole trip's been a waste of time. From the point of view of the case, I mean. A cross-section of England on a morning like this is a bonus,' he added as the Rover swept through the red-gold autumn leaves and silver trunks of beech woods. 'We've time enough. Let's stop at decent-looking places for coffee and some lunch.'

It was afternoon when they breasted a long rise and caught their first glimpse of Lodwick, a compact little town set in a dale, solid and self-contained. Toye, who had characteristically studied the AA book, made unerringly for the Golden Fleece, a two-star hostelry in the central square. It was warm and welcoming, with a log fire in the reception area and a faint background aroma of roast meat and a bar. Two rooms for the night were readily available. Pollard sensed that their arrival aroused interest and volunteered the information that they were on a business trip and would be leaving the

105

following morning, and relaxed briefly over an early cup of tea.

Pollard's surmise that The Grange, Mrs Ross's house, was one of the solid prosperous-looking dwellings that they had passed on their way into Lodwick, proved correct. Gates standing open gave on to a well-kept drive which curved round to a portico sheltering the front door of an eighteenth-century house of grey stone. The bell, he noticed, was the old-fashioned type which one had to pull. Footsteps sounded within, and an elderly woman, clearly a housekeeper, opened the door.

'You'll be the gentlemen from London,' she said, stating a fact rather than asking a question. 'The mistress is expecting you. Please come in.'

They stepped into an atmosphere of solid static comfort. Sound-deadening carpet covered the hall floor. A gentle warmth and faint fragrance of wood smoke came from a large stove on the left. Facing it was a handsome mahogany hatstand which had, no doubt, originally supported the late Mr Ross's assorted headgear. Two large panelled doors on each side of the hall presumably led to the main ground floor living-rooms, while in the far left corner a discreet green baize door suggested access to what, Pollard wondered, were still referred to as the servants' quarters. Immediately opposite the front door a broad staircase with highly-polished banisters rose some dozen steps before branching to right and left to give access to the first floor, vanishing into the dusk in the process.

The front door was closed behind them and without asking for their names the elderly woman led the way towards the door on the right immediately beyond the hatstand. As her hand went out to the handle Pollard got the impression of a slight movement on the landing overhead. The next moment the door was flung wide and their escort stood aside to let the two men pass.

'The gentlemen you're expecting, ma'am,' she announced, and promptly withdrew, closing the door behind her.

It was a beautiful room, its good proportions managing to assert themselves in spite of an overplus of heavy chintz-covered sofas and armchairs, and occasional tables laden with silver and photographs. Its only occupant sat in an armchair by the log fire and surveyed them.

'Detective-Chief Superintendent Pollard and Detective-Inspector Toye of New Scotland Yard?' she queried, making no attempt to rise. 'Forgive my remaining seated. My arthritis is rather troublesome today. Please find yourselves seats. I take it that Scotland Yard has been called in to investigate my nephew's murder because of this extraordinary affair of a letter bomb being sent to the Minstow officer who was in charge of the enquiry. Are these two facts thought to be connected?'

'Thank you, Mrs Ross,' Pollard replied taking a chair from which he faced her across the hearth. 'I can only tell you that at the moment we have no evidence about the sender.'

Toye stationed himself slightly to his superior's rear and came under scrutiny.

'Do you always hunt in couples?' she asked.

'When an important statement has been offered, and a homicide and possibly also an attempted homicide are involved, one needs a careful record. Among other things Inspector Toye is an expert stenographer.'

As he spoke he felt his attention alerted. This was a formidable woman. Physically dominating, to begin with. Even though she was seated, eighty-three years of age and a bit stiff in the joints, it was easy to see that

Grizel Ross was a tall, powerfully built woman. About five foot ten, he estimated, observing her strong shoulders, emphatic jaw and still abundant white hair drawn back and firmly secured in a bun. . . . Prototype of an efficient chairwoman of numerous committees, he thought. His conversation over the telephone with Inspector Tribe of the Northshire County Police came back to him, and he felt a sudden sympathy for Lodwick delinquents, non-churchgoers, the staff and pupils of the local school and anyone whose openly-expressed political views differed from Mrs Ross's. She was dressed for warmth and ease in a long housecoat of some dark red material which looked well-cut and expensive. An ebony walking stick with a silver crook handle hung easily accessible on the back of a small chair drawn up beside her. Their eyes met as they took each other's measure. Hers were clear and blue and to his intrigued surprise he recognised a glint of humour and understanding in them.

'For a start,' she said, 'do, please, jettison any idea that I want to provide information which may be relevant to John Paterson's death because of any affection for him. In my view he was a most unlikeable person. May this be put on record, please?'

'Certainly. Inspector Toye is taking a verbatim record of this interview.'

'Excellent. Perhaps I had better begin by giving you a brief outline of the Paterson family.'

'There is no need, Mrs Ross. Mr Bathurst, your late nephew's solicitor, has given us a genealogical table of the four generations from your father to your great-nephew. Get it out of the case file, would you, Inspector?'

Grizel Ross was clearly impressed.

'A further saving of time,' she said. 'A consideration

108

at my age. I shall now enlarge as briefly as possible on four members of the family. As far as my late nephew, John Paterson, goes I shall disregard the '*de mortuis*' precept and say frankly that he was a most unpleasant person. Able up to a point certainly. He had some reputation as a geologist, but Minstow College of Education is hardly Oxbridge, is it? He had a ludicrously exaggerated idea of his own importance and status, and a corresponding contempt for his colleagues with a particular aversion to the Deputy Head of his Department, a man called Grimshaw. I don't know why, but John was positively malicious about him.'

She paused. Pollard was conscious of Toye's pen, arrested and poised over his notebook. A log fell apart in the fire, sending up a shower of sparks.

'My niece Morag,' she resumed, 'was a silly girl with no judgement, and made a poor match to a teacher of chemistry called Forbes. They were both killed in a motoring accident when their som Mark was eight years old. His future was something of a problem. John, with his characteristic selfishness, washed his hands of the whole business, and at the time I was much pre-occupied with my local commitments and my husband's health. In the end my brother Hamish set up a trust for the boy's maintenance and education, and his father's sister and her husband brought Mark up. Hamish died soon afterwards, leaving a life interest in the family money to John with ultimate reversion to Mark, who was sent to a minor public school. Apart from an interest in science his work was of a very average standard, and he had no wish to go on to a university. However, he has at least held down his first job – with Iremongers, the big property agents – and is making his way in the firm. But at twenty-two he made a most unsuitable marriage which has just broken up. He is also extravagant in his living standards, and to save his job with Iremongers I was recently obliged to pay his debts, but I made it clear that it was for the first and last time.'

'Have you recently seen much of both Dr Paterson and Mark Forbes?' Pollard asked, wondering if he would ever get down to the purpose of his visit.

Grizel Ross gave him an openly amused glance.

'I really am coming to the point, Chief Superintendent. My husband died in 1970, leaving his quite substantial personal fortune to me absolutely. To my surprise – and frank amusement – John Paterson who had not been near me for years suddenly proposed himself as a visitor, and has continued to pay me mercifully brief visits annually. Mark had been sent to see me at intervals during his younger days, and of recent years these visits have become much more frequent. He was here for several days last July, and I had a telephone call from him yesterday asking for a bed for tonight. The motives behind this sudden attentiveness need hardly be pointed out to you: both John and Mark are at pains to make me fully aware of their existence, and to find out if they possibly can how I intend to leave my money.'

Pollard found himself unable to refrain from returning the smile which accompanied these remarks. . . . An old tartar, he thought, but I like her. Patently dead straight. . . .

'Now at long last,' she went on, 'I'm coming to the matter which made me feel it was my moral duty to contact the police in connection with John Paterson's murder. About a year ago I came to the conclusion that I needed a resident companion. Not to be constantly with me, heaven forbid, but for odd jobs about the house and driving me to church and so on. For many years I have supported an excellent orphanage which not only sees to

110

it that their children get a good basic education but follows this with having them trained for any work they would like to take up. I asked them if they could recommend one of their old girls and they sent me Jean Naylor. She is twenty-seven, a State Enrolled Nurse and quite bearable to have in the house. I have done all I could to help her join in Lodwick activities, had her taught to drive my car and encouraged her to make reasonable personal use of it, and so forth. . . . However, Chief Superintendent, I was on our local Bench for many years and have been involved in social work of various kinds, and seen something of children and adolescents brought up 'in care' for one reason or another. The 'care' can be admirable, but its charges practically always carry over into adult life some degree of an inferiority complex and a sense of insecurity. Jean came of respectable working-class stock but was orphaned young and had no near relatives prepared to take her on. Harringtons – the orphanage I was speaking about – tried to get her happily adopted, but after a couple of attempts which ended in failure they kept her with them. In due course she chose a nurse's training and qualified as an SEN, the SRN qualification being too difficult for her. After a couple of hospital jobs she told the Director of Harringtons – they are very good at keeping in touch with their former charges – that she would like to try a private nursing job, and so she came to me.'

At this point Grizel Ross paused, and asked Toye to put some more logs on the fire. Pollard sensed that she was finding the next instalment of her statement an effort, and wondered what could possibly be coming.

'Thank you, Inspector,' she said, as Toye went back to his chair. 'To continue,' she resumed, 'Jean settled quickly here, and after a few weeks told me rather

111

pathetically that she had never been so happy, but all the same I could still detect her latent sense of insecurity. It showed in things like a rather excessive desire to please, for instance, and undue curiosity about things that were no concern of hers. Obviously sooner or later some minor frictions were bound to crop up. One day at the end of June she made a tiresome muddle over some shopping and I was sharp with her for the first time. I was having rather a bad day with my arthritis, although this is an explanation, not an excuse. Jean was very upset and apprehensive for some days. I cast around for something to restore her confidence and remembered that she had several times spoken of a friend, also a Harrington girl now married, and thought it might be a good move to ask Jean if she would like to invite this friend to come here on a visit for a few days at some future date, and take her for some drives and so on. I casually asked her name and learnt that it was now Linda Grimshaw, and that her husband was a lecturer in a college at a place in southern England called Minstow.'

Pollard watched Toye's pen suddenly suspended over his notebook, and looked up to meet Grizel Ross's steady gaze.

'We've almost arrived, Chief Superintendent,' she said. 'At first I merely took the marriage as an odd coincidence, but wrote to the Director of Harringtons to ask him if this friendship was a good thing for Jean. He replied that Linda Grimshaw had always been perfectly satisfactory. Here is his reply to my letter which I feel you should read.'

She took an envelope from a handbag and passed it to Pollard. It carried the printed heading HARRING-TONS, EASTCLIFF, NORTHSHIRE, and 'Personal' was handwritten in the top left-hand corner.

'. . . In answer to your enquiry about Linda

112

Hawkins,' the Director wrote, 'she is one of our success stories, doing well here and at school, and subsequently qualifying as a shorthand-typist. She is married to a college lecturer at Minstow in the south and is now Linda Grimshaw. Because of your long and generous association with us I feel justified in telling you a little more about her background. She is illegitimate, born in 1953 at Wringtonford to Sarah Hawkins, spinster and an unknown father. The mother rented a room in the city, and had a series of casual jobs. She was suspected by the police of occasional soliciting but no charge was ever made. She died when Linda was four. The Wringtonford welfare people were unable to trace the Hawkins family, or, of course, the unknown father, although after Sarah Hawkins's death they went through her few possessions and something came to light which they passed on to us when we took over Linda. One was the child's birth certificate. Someone –presumably Sarah – had crossed out 'father unknown' and written above it 'John Hamish Paterson'. We took advice, and the upshot was that no attempt was made to trace this man. Four years had elapsed since Linda's birth, and as you know, Paterson is a name which is not uncommon in the North. All this was before my appointment, of course, but after I came I went through our 'Highly Confidential' file. I may add that Linda knows nothing of the matter. When she reached the stage of asking about her parents I showed her a fresh duplicate copy of her birth certificate which we had obtained from the authorties.'

When Pollard had finished reading the letter he handed it to Toye without comment. Finally Grizel Ross broke the silence.

'I know perfectly well what you are going to say, Chief Superintendent,' she said. 'That this is not conclusive evidence that Linda Grimshaw is my illegitimate great-niece. It is possible that the 'John Hamish Paterson' inserted on the original birth certificate is not my late nephew John Hamish Paterson. But the letter from the Director was startling, all the same. There was at the time a branch of my father's textile manufacturing firm at Wringtonford, and as a young man with scientific interests John used to visit the works at intervals. A day or two later when I was mulling over the situation it suddenly struck me that the letter had been a long time in reaching me. Even now letters from Harringtons almost always arrive in two days. I had kept this particular one in its envelope which was dated and post-marked 4 July but it did not reach me until the 8th. One of Jean's duties is to bring my letters up to my bedroom as soon as the mail arrives. Then I looked at the back of the envelope. Would you do the same? There's a powerful magnifying glass on the bureau over there, Inspector,'

Toye got up, fetched it and handed it to Pollard who moved across the room to stand under the full light of a standard lamp. He scrutinised the back of the envelope which had been cut open neatly at the top leaving the flap sealed down. Finally he sniffed the flap.

'It's impossible to be absolutely definite without tests in a forensic laboratory,' he told Grizel Ross, 'but I think that this envelope was steamed open and afterwards resealed with an adhesive.'

Toye concurred after examining the envelope himself.

'My own conclusion' Grizel Ross said. 'My reconstruction of what happened is this. The upset with Jean I told you about was on 27 June. The next day I happened to write to the Director of Harringtons about a totally different matter, not mentioning Jean at all. She takes my letters to the post, and would have noticed

114

the address and jumped to the conclusion that I had written to say that I was finding her unsuitable and that she must go. She also brings my morning mail up to my bedroom. As you see, letters from Harringtons have an official heading on their envelopes. I think that she was finding her entirely unnecessary anxiety about her future so unbearable, poor child, that she abstracted the Director's reply to my letter, steamed open the envelope and read it. John has stayed here, and she would have seen his signature 'J.H. Paterson' in my visitors' book. I do not think her friendship with Linda Grimshaw is a very intimate one but she must know something of the difficulties between her husband and my late nephew. She now had a most interesting piece of information to pass on when Linda's proposed visit took place. Much more exciting to tell her by word of mouth than in a letter, of course.

'Before I had made up my mind whether or not I should tackle her about opening the letter, I had a telephone call from Mark Forbes. He was coming to these parts on his firm's business and asked if he could stay here for two or three nights in the middle of July. I agreed, not without certain sardonic thoughts, and he duly turned up.

'As I said just now, one way in which Jean shows her sense of insecurity is by trying too hard to please. Mark, who cannot refrain from exercising what he considers his personal charm on any female, soon had her eating out of his hand as the saying is. He had an afternoon to spare and asked if he might take her for a drive. I did not like the idea at all, but felt that after what had happened between her and myself it would be bad psychological handling to refuse. So they went off.'

'And you deduce,' Pollard asked, 'that in the course of conversation about your nephew John Paterson's visits, perhaps, Jean talked about the contents of the Harrington letter?'

'Exactly. And I think Mark probably advised her to keep it to herself for fear of distressing her friend, while planning to ingratiate himself with John by giving him a powerful weapon against the unfortunate Mr Grimshaw.

'And you suggest,' Pollard said thoughtfully, 'that this weapon was in due course used, and Grimshaw, to protect Linda from knowing that Paterson was her father, decided to liquidate him?'

'I do.' As she spoke, Grizel pressed a bell in the wall beside her. 'I'm going up to bed now, I'm tired after this long talk. My housekeeper will give me any help I need, I'll send Jean down to you. Get it out of her about opening the letter, but for pity's sake convince her that I understood why she did it, and am not in the least angry with her. And anyone as acute as you are won't find it difficult to find out if she told Mark its contents. . . . Ah, here you are, Annie. I want you to get me to bed while these gentlemen have a word with Jean. . . .'

She allowed Pollard to help her up and after saying goodbye to Toye and himself, walked slowly on her housekeeper's arm to the door. As a Parthian shot she glanced over her shoulder with a look of amusement.

'My bark, Chief Superintendent,' she observed, 'as you may have noticed, is worse than my bite.'

As the door closed the two men sank into their chairs and looked at each other, Pollard remarking that he had never expected the plot to thicken to this extent. Voices in the hall were faintly audible. A moment or two later there was a hesitant fumbling at the door handle and a slight figure in a tweed skirt and blue polo-necked jumper came uncertainly into the room. Pollard and Toye got up again.

116

'Miss Naylor, isn't it?' Pollard said in a relaxed tone. 'Do come and sit down. You know, I'm sure, that Inspector Toye and I are from Scotland Yard, and are investigating the murder of Mrs Ross's nephew Dr John Paterson.'

'Yes,' she replied, almost inaudibly, sitting upright in her chair and twisting her hands together. She was at any rate at this moment, pale, with mousey and slightly curly hair, brown eyes and a rather small face with unemphatic features. The sort of face that made so little impression on you that it would be difficult to remember it accurately, Pollard thought. He had a natural flair for playing his professional interviews by ear, and decided to plunge straight in.

'An impolite question to ask a lady,' he said, 'but how old are you, Miss Naylor?'

'Twenty-seven.'

She looked younger, apart from what seemed to be a permanent slight furrow of anxiety between her eyes. Rather over-shadowed by the size of the room and the somewhat stuffy opulence of its furnishings. . . .

'You were left an orphan quite young, weren't you and went to live at Harringtons? And you've got the usual "thing" about having been brought up in an orphanage – that it somehow makes you a second-class citizen? That's why you're so very lucky to have landed up here, Miss Naylor, with somebody like Mrs Ross who understands just how you feel. And that is why you just *had* to open that letter the Director of Harringtons wrote to her, to make sure that she wasn't going to give you the sack, because she'd been annoyed with you about some shopping?'

Jean Naylor's hand flew to her mouth. She stared at Pollard in speechless horror.

'She's found out?' she gasped at last.

117

'Why yes. You didn't make much of a job of sticking it up again, you know. And the date of the letter and the date it reached Mrs Ross didn't match up.'

The latter possibility had obviously never occurred to her. She's decidedly limited, Pollard thought.

'What's going to happen?' she said rather faintly.

'What I hope is going to happen is that you're going to see things much more sensibly. You read the newspapers I expect, don't you?'

Jean Naylor nodded in bewilderment.

'Well then, you know that there are children who weren't wanted, or who only have one parent or who get passed on from one person to another and so on. Those are the children who really are in danger of being second-class citizens when they grow up, not those who go to a place like Harringtons which cares about its children and does everything possible to give them a good start in life like your hospital training. You're a qualified SEN, aren't you? That's something worthwhile that you can be proud of.'

'I hadn't thought about all that,' she said slowly.

'And then there's Mrs Ross. She's old and often in pain and needs you. She feels lonely without her husband, I'm sure. She doesn't see very much of her great-nephew, Mr Mark Forbes, does she?'

Jean blushed slightly.

'He stays here when he's anywhere near, inspecting property for the company he works for. Last July he was here for five days and took me for a wonderful drive, and we stopped for tea at a big hotel. It's such a lovely car. And he's unexpectedly coming late tonight,' she added, her eyes brightening at the prospect.

'He sounds one of those friendly people who are easy to talk to,' Pollard remarked. 'Perhaps it was rather a relief to tell him about the bit of bother you had with his

118

great aunt, and how you were so worried that she might have written to Harrington's to say she didn't want to keep you on that you simply had to open their answer and find out.'

'Well, I did,' Jean admitted with a blush. 'I was feeling so bad about it and there wasn't anyone else to talk to. You see, I can't help feeling just a bit envious of Linda. She's got a husband who lectures in a college, and they've a car. She's got a much grander sort of life than mine. Why, she was going to drive herself to a friend's wedding and staying in the house, even though it meant leaving Ron at the beginning of the College half-term week and not getting back till the Sunday. Mark – he said I was to call him that – was so interested about Linda and who she really is, but he said it wouldn't be wise to tell her because I'd be giving myself away about having opened the letter. I hadn't thought of that, so of course I said I never would,' she ended näively.

'You didn't tell Dr Paterson when he came up here to stay in the autumn that you knew he'd been a bit of a lad in his younger days?' Pollard enquired jocularly.

Jean Naylor looked horrorstruck at the suggestion.

'Oh, *no*. I'd never have dared. He hardly seemed to notice that I was here, and practically never spoke to me. Of course I'm sorry somebody killed him in that dreadful way, but I didn't like him a bit. And you could see Mrs Ross didn't care much for him.'

Pollard decided that he had extracted all the information that Jean Naylor had to offer, and brought the interview to an end by way of a few general topics. Finally he extracted a promise from her that she would go straight up and have a talk with Mrs Ross and be absolutely frank about the Harrington letter. To his surprise when he and Toye rose to leave she rang the bell.

'Annie always shows visitors out,' she explained.

'Lumme,' Toye commented as the front door closed behind them. 'Well, it points to Forbes telling Paterson, and Paterson not being able to resist ramming it down Grimshaw's throat that Friday afternoon. If he did, I reckon Paterson asked for what he got the next day.'

'I'm inclined to agree,' Pollard replied as they made their way to the Golden Fleece. 'Another possibility is that Forbes saw a promising blackmailing gambit in Jean Naylor's guileless disclosure. I wonder how Forbes will react when he turns up tonight and hears we've been on the trail up here.'

Chapter Eight

On the drive up to Lodwick, Pollard had noticed a turn-off to Hollowcombe. It brought back to his mind the part this place had played in connection with his big case in the preceding summer. An entry in its parish registers had been an important clue. He remembered that its church had some exceptionally fine mediaeval glass, an art form in which his artist wife Jane was interested. Over breakfast on the following morning he broached the subject of a brief diversion to Toye. As he had expected, the latter's initial response was rather muted. As a staunch Evangelical he disapproved of anything ornate in a church building, and would see the suggested diversion as a departure from the straight and narrow path of professional duty which demanded their immediate return to Minstow. However, his high regard for Jane Pollard as wife, mother and artist enabled him to square his conscience. Pollard pointed out that they were making a very early start instead of having an extra hour's kip, and they duly set off in harmony.

Hollowdale turned out to be a thriving market town with quite a large church. On going inside Pollard took a quick look round and detected some traces of an earlier Norman building, but there had been extensive rebuilding and enlargement in the late fourteenth century. An unusual quantity of mediaeval glass had survived the attentions of iconoclasts inspired by various motives. Pollard gazed with admiration at the splendid reds and blues in the heavily leaded panes of the earlier windows, and the transition to the predominant yellows of all shades in the later ones which were less striking, but certainly admitted more light and were more varied in theme. He spared a few moments to look at the magnificent screen, and the joined Toye who was studying the Visitors' Book on a table near the south door. There seemed to be a remarkable number of visitors for a remote church, many of whom would probably have come to see the glass. There were three columns in the book headed respectively Name, Address and Comments. Apart from one or two childish attempts at humour these latter were often informed and invariably complimentary both to the church and of its standard of maintenance. Pollard suddenly broke off while entering his own address and turned to Toye.

'Something hit me,' he said. 'That couple Grimshaw told Nevinson he met at the abandoned village . . . Didn't he say he'd told them the best things to go and see in Minstow? Some of them might have Visitors' Books like this, and its just possible we might get on to their address. There can't have been all that number of couples sightseeing in Minstow on 21 October.'

They stood and looked at each other.

'Could be a breakthrough,' Toye allowed with characteristic caution. 'They'd go to the Cathedral, but there wouldn't be a Visitors' Book there. Too many people coming and going. But Minstow's an old city and I'd be surprised if there aren't some other show places.'

'Here, sign on the dotted line,' Pollard said, pushing the book towards him, having finished entering his own

122

address and adding an enthusiastic if somewhat illegible remark. 'And let's go. Grimshaw's alibi is a top priority after what we've learnt up here.'

Five minutes later they were heading south in the Rover.

They ran into Minstow in mid-afternoon and went straight to the police station. Superintendent Lock was out on a case and they were received by Sergeant Andrews. He looked portentous and clearly had information to impart. After considering likely early callers at Loyes Cottage he had run to earth the postman on the early delivery round of 21 October. This man, Jim Bagnall, had met the Mini and the Caravette driving down the cul-de-sac to the main road as he was coming up it on his push bike with the mail for Loyes Cottage. There wasn't much room to pass so he jumped off his bike and kept well into the hedge. The gent driving the brown Mini had raised his hand polite-like, but Dr Paterson seemed to be looking for something in the glove compartment and hardly bothered, even though Bagnall waved his mail at him. Andrews had gathered that Paterson was not popular with delivery men and stingy as hell when it came to Christmas boxes.

Asked about the time of the encounter, Bagnall was definite that it had not been more than two or three minutes past nine. He'd been well on schedule with deliveries that morning.

Pollard congratulated Andrews on getting Mark Forbes's statement on the time of departure from Loyes Cottage so definitely corroborated.

'Any other luck?' he asked.

It appeared that a young Little Underhill boy had noticed a Jaguar going through the village towards the London road later that morning, but was too vague about the time for this information to be of any value.

Nobody at the farm at the bottom of Twisterdown had seen a hiker going up the track between 8.30 and 9 o'clock that morning, but the farmer himself had noticed a couple going down towards the road after dinner. He couldn't be sure of the time except that it was somewhere in the middle of the afternoon.

'Too late,' Pollard said. 'The couple we're interested in would have wanted some grub long before then.'

He described the morning's visit to Hollowdale church and the idea that had struck him while he had been signing the Visitors' Book. However, when asked what places of interest in Minstow besides the Cathedral would be likely to attract tourists, Sergeant Andrews seemed at a loss. He was obviously one of the many who are surprisingly ignorant of features of interest on their home ground. After Pollard had provisionally rejected the Museum and the Art Gallery he scratched his head and finally came up with the Bridge Chapel.

'It's a funny little place at the south end of the old bridge that's closed for traffic now,' he said, 'and there's a preservation order on it, so when there was talk of widening the bridge way back after the War they found it wasn't on.'

'Thank God for that, anyway,' Pollard said. 'Do visitors go to see this chapel?'

'Yes, sir. Any number of 'em. I've never been inside myself, but I've heard it said it's mentioned in books on old buildings. It's only open at certain times, though. There's a board outside giving them.'

'Who's responsible for it? I mean, is it Church property or City Council property?'

Sergeant Andrews did not know. Pollard thought briefly and asked to be put through to the Archdeacon of Minstow. On introducing himself he sensed intense interest at the other end of the line.

'Of course I know why you're down here,' a brisk pleasant voice told him, 'but I can't imagine how I come in. Do tell me.'

Pollard did so, and the facts he wanted were immediately forthcoming. Bridge Chapel had obviously once been a place of Christian worship, probably used by travellers entering or leaving the city. After the Reformation it apparently fell into disuse and by Georgian times was in a ruinous state. In the nineteenth century the growing interest in the past had led to its restoration by zealous local antiquarians, and it had eventually passed into the ownership of the City Council together with the Old Bridge. The latter was closed to wheeled traffic in the 1950s as soon as the modern bridge had been completed. With the growth of tourism after the Second World War the Council realised that they had a potential asset in the chapel which was given a facelift, and now brought in a modest income for purposes described as *Maintenance and Preservation of this Historic Building.*

'There's no charge for admission,' the Archdeacon said 'but it's quite surprising what people put into the collecting box. And there's a small illustrated pamphlet on sale and a picture postcard of the place.'

'Is there a Visitors' Book?' Pollard asked, and found himself momentarily holding his breath.

'Yes. I took some visiting friends along about a month ago, and remember their signing it.'

'It's that book I want to have a look at. I imagine the City Council offices will have packed it in for the day. Can you advise me who to contact?'

'I think the best thing would be for me to ring Edward Boycott, the Chairman of the City Council's Estates and Properties Sub-Committee and find out how you can get hold of the key. I'll get him to ring you direct at the police station. How's that?'

'It sounds first rate, Archdeacon, and I'm most grateful to you.'

'The gratitude's on my side, I assure you, Chief Superintendent. It's quite something to be asked to co-operate with Scotland Yard.'

Pollard and Toye spent the interval while waiting for the call in making a start on compiling a report of their visit to Lodwick. In a short time Mr Boycott was on the line and as obviously intrigued and ready to be helpful as the Archdeacon. He undertook to ring the night porter at the Council Offices and instruct him to hand over the key of Bridge Chapel to the police who would be calling for it. Pollard thanked him, undertook to return the key within an hour and tactfully brought the conversation to an end.

'Come on,' he said to Toye. 'Let's rustle up some torches in case there's no lighting and go along straight away.'

Toye had already consulted a street plan and found that Old Bridge was a bare ten minutes' walk from the police station, allowing for collecting the key from the Council Offices on the way. They found the entrance to the bridge firmly blocked off for cars by a row of bollards, and on passing through these came almost at once to a small rectangular building on the right of the road. A noticeboard outside announced that Bridge Chapel was open to the public free of charge from 2.30 to 5.30 p.m., daily from 1 March to 1 October, and on Wednesdays and Saturdays during the winter months.

'That,' Pollard commented as Toye manipulated an enormous key, 'could be our second break today. Wednesdays and Saturdays.'

Rather to his surprise the tiny chapel had atmosphere, even though a good deal of space was taken up by a table and chair for the custodian on duty. There were bare

126

stone walls, relieved only by a framed inscription of what was surmised and known of the building's history. Opposite the door was what appeared to be the base of a former small stone altar. Tiny windows looking along the bridge and towards the city were protected by exterior iron grilles. On the table was the collecting box for voluntary contributions mentioned by the Archdeacon, together with pamphlets and postcards and a leatherbound book measuring roughly 6 inches by 8 and inscribed 'VISITORS' in gold lettering. Its pages were ruled into columns with headings similar to those at Hollowdale. Pollard and Toye looked down on three separate entries for 21 October.

Harley F. and Lucille Wendell. White Cross, Vermont. U.S.A.

Bill and Babs Haraway, Tommy and Jane. 5 Market Street, Midlake, Longshire

John and Ruth Penfold, 302 London Road, Warhampton, North Midlands

'Third time lucky?' queries Pollard. 'Grimshaw would have said if they were Yanks or had a couple of kids with them. If he really met up with them, that is.'

'Could be,' Toye soberly replied, copying down all three entries. Pollard, visited by a hunch, put a generous contribution into the collecting box.

They locked up the little chapel carefully and returned the key to the Council Offices on their way back to the police station. Sensing the question in Toye's mind Pollard announced that he had decided against contacting the Penfolds by telephone.

'They're our best – if not our only – lead at the moment,' he said. 'Spontaneous reactions to un-expected questions often pay off, don't they? And I realised last night that I'd missed out on my godson's first birthday last weekend, and I'm dropping in with a

127

present before we start off, come hell or high water. It's his dad's birthday, too, so there's a good excuse to take along a bottle for Nevinson.'

After a long overdue meal at the George and Dragon they compiled a report on the visit to Lodwick and the discovery of the Penfolds' address. Finally Pollard rang Jane at their Wimbledon home, telling her that he would be driving up to the Midlands on the following morning, but with any luck he would be home for supper and for the night.

'How's the going?' she asked, using their motoring code.

'Some unexpected diversions from the route we expected to take,' he said.

The next day they breakfasted early and briefly went their separate ways. Toye took the Rover once again to the garage which had met with his approval for petrol and a tyre check. Pollard collected two bottles of sherry and a wooden elephant on wheels which he had purchased in advance. His arrival at the Nevinsons' house created a furore. Charles had been sent home from hospital and Pollard managed in the general jubilation to convey to him that an unexpected and quite promising lead had turned up, involving an immediate visit to Warhampton.

'You shall have the whole bloody case from A to Z when it's tied up,' he promised.

The contact with the Nevinsons and a crisp autumn morning made him feel optimistic. As the miles fell away behind them he sat for some time mentally reviewing the case and studying Ordnance Survey maps of the Minstow area.

'The fact that the farmer bloke says he saw a couple of

hikers coming down from Twisterdown some time during the afternoon could be important after all,' he said, suddenly breaking the silence.

'Meaning,' Toye asked, dexterously overtaking a long vehicle, 'that Grimshaw might have arrived at this old-time village place much later than he says he did? Having somehow been at Durnycombe shoving the Caravette over the cliff. But unless the shopkeeper's lying he was buying a slab of chocolate near Rosemary Close at about 8.40 that morning. Andrews checked up on that. How could Grimshaw have got to Durnycombe by the time Paterson arrived there round 10 o'clock? He hadn't a car. Forbes arrived about five past, so if Grimshaw did the job it must have been done by then.

Pollard searched in the case file to find Charles Nevinson's timetable of the comings and goings involving Grey's Garage.

'Elementary, my dear Watson,' he said after a brief scrutiny. 'We ought to have got on to this before. It's roughly eleven miles from Minstow to Durnycombe, and a good level road with a decent surface until you turn off for the cliffs. Grimshaw could have done it on a good push bike between 8.45 and 9.50 say. Nevinson estimates Paterson's time of passing Grey's Garage as 9.45, and it's eight minutes by car from there to Durnycombe. The Caravette might have been a bit slower. Three new lines of enquiry open up. Has Grimshaw got a push bike? If not, has one been reported missing? And did anybody notice a chap pedalling energetically along the Minstow-Coryport road in the direction of Coryport between 8.45 and 9.45 that Saturday morning? If the Penfolds say they didn't meet up with a bloke on the village site until about a quarter to two we'll ring Super Lock from Warhampton and ask him to get enquiries going.'

'You can't fault all that as far as it goes,' Toye allowed, 'but how did he get back to Twisterdown and all but up to the top by the time the Penfolds arrived?'

'Pull into this lay-by,' Pollard told him, 'and have a look at the map. Say he sent the Caravette over at 10 approx., what's the earliest time he could have got to Twisterdown by the Regional Coastal Path from Durnycombe?'

They studied the relevant sheet of the 1:25000 Ordnance Survey map carefully, observing the steepness of the gradients and finally measuring the route as accurately as they could with a length of fine string.

'About a mile and a half longer than the road,' Toye said, 'with all the ins and outs of the coastline, and mighty rough going. Not far short of a dozen miles. I reckon he couldn't possibly have made it on foot under four hours.'

'My estimate exactly,' Pollard agreed. 'So he wouldn't have got to the village site till 2 at the earliest. Possibly later. That would mean that the Penfolds – if they were the hikers the farmer saw – wouldn't have got down until about 3.30, if then. A bit late for what you'd call mid-afternoon, perhaps. Of course if he'd biked from Minstow, in theory he could have biked back to Twisterdown along the coastal path in – say –two and a half hours, but there are terrific hills on that stretch, and he'd probably have had half a dozen punctures en route. If he biked out to Durnycombe I'd expect him to chuck the thing over the cliff and go all out on foot for Twisterdown, but we'd better have a search made for a discarded bike.'

'Good I'll buy all that, Chief,' Toye commented, looking at Pollard with unconcealed admiration. 'What with that idea you got from the Visitors' Book up at

130

Hollowdale and then the push bike and these maps I reckon it's going to be one of your biggest scoops yet.'

'Don't tempt providence, old man. It all depends on these Penfolds. Let's push on and hope they're at home and not off on another hike. Our footwear wouldn't be suitable for a follow-on.'

On arrival at Warhampton they drove straight to police headquarters where Pollard presented his credentials to a startled duty sergeant. He had given advance notice of his visit and was promptly ushered into the Chief Superintendent of the city CID.

'We don't often get quite such a distinguished visitor,' the latter said as they shook hands. 'What can we do for you?'

'I won't take up more than a few minutes of your time,' Pollard told him. 'We've come up to get confirmation or not of a statement by a Mr and Mrs Penfold of 302 London Road. An entry in a Visitors' Book dated 21 October, actually.'

Superintendent Baring's eyes widened.

'I saw in the press that Minstow had asked the Yard to come in after somebody sent their chap a letter bomb. . . . However, to answer your implied question, the Penfolds are a hundred per cent. John Penfold's a senior partner in Warhampton's leading firm of solicitors. Highly intelligent and sea-green incorruptible, and so's his wife. Keen conservationists, both of them, and they'd be ideal witnesses if your case comes to court. How's it going?'

Pollard grinned.

'Ever built a house of cards?' he asked.

'Sure. I was quite a dab at it when I was a lad.'

'One puff from the Penfolds and mine collapses. I'm keeping my fingers crossed.'

'Like that, is it?'

131

Inevitably Chief Superintendent Baring's curiosity had to be gratified to some extent, but Pollard got away as soon as he respectably could. Toye, waiting in the car park, had meanwhile got instructions on the shortest route to the London road out of the city. Progressive expansion of Warhampton had produced an interesting succession of changes in domestic architecture over the years. Number 302 appeared to be of the between-the-wars vintage, solidly built in brick which had mellowed and was set in a moderately large garden. The garage doors were open, and the sight of a car inside was encouraging. Presumably the owners were at home.

The middle-aged man who came to the front door was wearing ancient slacks, a grey pullover and slippers. He was holding a book with his finger inserted to keep his place and looked at his visitors enquiringly.

'Mr Penfold?' Pollard queried holding out his official card. 'Sorry to disturb you.'

The card received a quick comprehensive glance and was handed back.

'John Penfold it is. I realise what you've come about, of course. Do come in, Chief Superintendent. I wonder how you've managed to run us to earth,' he added, leading the way into a sitting-room at the back of the house. A woman also wearing slacks and a pullover rose from the depths of a comfortable chair by a small log fire.

'My wife, Gentlemen. We both freely admit to having been in the area of the crime on Saturday 21 October, don't we, darling? Meet Detective-Chief Super-intendent Pollard of New Scotland Yard and . . . ?'

'Detective-Inspector Toye,' Pollard supplied.

Mrs Penfold had straight no-nonsense bobbed hair, a very intelligent face and an attractive smile.

'This is the sort of thing that happens to people in

132

books and films,' she said. 'It's thrilling, but I simply can't imagine how you've found us. Do sit down.'

As they all did so her husband brought down his hand on the cover of the book he was still holding.

'Got it!' he said. 'We signed the Visitors' Book in that little chapel on the old bridge at Minstow.'

'Congratulations,' Pollard replied. 'You should be in the CID, Mr Penfold. Actually, I think you can help us considerably. Would you give us as detailed an account as you can of how you spent that Saturday, say up to the time when you arrived in Minstow. It's detailed timing we're interested in.'

'We'll do our best, although the idea was to get a break from clocks and timekeeping. We'd each kept a week of our holidays for an autumn break and took it from Saturday 14 October to Sunday 22nd. We enjoy walking and are gradually doing what there is of the National Coastal Path, and this time decided on the stretch between Westermouth and Coryport. We drove to Westermouth on the 14th, left the car in a garage and started off the next day. The fine weather we've had this autumn held up, and we took it easy, covering about fifteen miles a day, and putting up for the nights in village pubs near the coast. We were at the Barley Mow in a little place called St Osric on the night of the 20th, and started off again after breakfast on the 21st. . . . Am I being too detailed?'

'No,' Pollard told him. 'From now on we'd like even more detail.' He glanced at Toye who had an Ordnance map open and was making a shorthand record.

'What time would you say we left the pub that morning?' Jonn Penfold asked his wife. '9.30?'

'9.30, near enough,' Caroline Penfold said. 'You remember we'd decided to have a snack in Minstow, and didn't ask for sandwiches to be put up.'

133

'Agreed. So we stepped out, heading for Minstow.'

Years of close collaboration had established a degree of telepathy between Pollard and Toye. . . . We've had it, Pollard thought. Much too early . . . it's going to tie up with Grimshaw's statement. . . .

'Did you meet anyone on the path?' he asked.

'Not a soul. The first sign of life was through binoculars from the top of Twisterdown, at about half-past eleven. It looked like a small party in the far distance, coming from the Coryport direction. Then when we turned off the path to make our way down to Minstow we saw a man lower down the slope who seemed to be pacing out distances and making notes. Our route down went past him, so we stopped to pass the time of day. He said he was investigating the site of an abandoned village that had shown up in a recent air photograph.'

'Would you describe him as accurately as you can?'

John Penfold leant back in his chair and clasped his hands behind his head.

'In his middle thirties, I should think. Average height. Light brown hair, a bit on the long side. Grey eyes. Standard shabby jeans and one of those short waterproof coats. Intelligent face, but the thing that struck me about him was that he looked absolutely all in.'

'Would you go along with that, Mrs Penfold?' Pollard enquired.

'Yes. I remember thinking that he couldn't be very fit if the climb up from Minstow had taken it out of him so much. I assumed, unreasonably perhaps, that he'd come from there. He might have walked from Coryport along the cliff path, or been ahead of us coming from the St Osric direction. I suppose.'

'Quite. Had he a lot of gear with him?'

134

'There was a rucksack on the ground with maps and notebooks spilling out of it, but he didn't seem to have got very far with the rough sketch of the site that he was making. It obviously is an abandoned village. I'm rather interested in that sort of thing myself. But he didn't seem keen to talk about it so we pushed on quite quickly.'

'What time was it when you left him?' Pollard asked, depressingly conscious of already knowing the answer.

'I can be absolutely definite about that,' John Penfold came in. 'I remember looking at my watch and wondering how long it would take to make Minstow. It was a quarter to twelve exactly.'

'Thank you,' Pollard said, watching Toye entering this statement in his notebook. 'You've given us some valuable information. We needn't bother you to carry on any further. It's possible that you may be called upon to give evidence at some future date.'

Both the Penfolds registered interest tempered with discretion. John Penfold added that he and his wife had been catching up on the Paterson case in the papers after lunch, and had decided to go along to the Warhampton police that evening and report their encounter with a man on the site of the abandoned village on Twisterdown.

'Needless to say we shall be following the progress of your case,' Mrs Penfold told him. 'As presumably we're not suspects may we offer you both a cup of tea?'

Pollard thanked her, but declined on the grounds that they were *en route* for the Yard. A few minutes later the Rover moved off Londonwards.

'So that's bloody well that,' Pollard said. 'Total collapse of what looked like a really promising lead. And for God's sake don't ask me where we go from here because I haven't a clue.'

*　　　*　　　*

On arrival at the Yard Pollard found reports of information collected at his request on John Paterson and Mark Forbes and settled down to study them without much optimism. Paterson's dramatic end had been given prominence in the press and the media's news programmes, and information about him had been comparatively easy to obtain. He had regularly attended London meetings and conferences of geological interest, and on these occasions and other unspecified ones had invariably stayed at one of the West End's largest and most impersonal hotels. Members of its staff, their memories refreshed by newspaper photographs described him as curt and tight-fisted. Enquiries further afield revealed visits over the years to a flat in the Maida Vale area in which the police were interested, but not to the point of taking any action.

Enquiries about Mark Forbes called for subtler methods and great expertise. The impressive head office of Iremonger Properties was approached in connection with a fictitious car accident of which Mr Mark Forbes was believed to have been a witness. Detective-Constable Chandler who had remarkable ability for extracting information from persons without their being aware of it contrived to get access to his secretary, a with-it blonde. Not that in his opinion she had been a blonde for long. It was necessary to consult Mr Forbes' engagement diary and she contrived to make this a protracted operation. . . .

'Looks as though he's a worker,' Chandler commented.

'That's right. Always in before zero hour: 9 a.m. that is. Good at sizing up properties from the point of view of the firm's profits, but it's felt in some quarters that he pushes a bit too hard, if you get me. He's got his sights on a partnership, of course, but you don't get one for the

136

asking in this set-up. There's a rumour going round that the murdered uncle was pretty warm, so maybe we'll be seeing things happening. It's the only thing that makes me hang on. Partners' secretaries get a sight more in their pay packets than I'm taking home.'

'What with the murder and his marriage busting up he can't have been all that easy to work with lately.'

'You're telling me. All tensed up and on edge and every time you open your mouth you put a foot wrong, especially since the murder. Of course having to go down to Minstow for the inquest and whatever put him behind with his work, and that doesn't suit a high flyer like him. The bosses here aren't too keen on the staff asking for extra leave . . .'

On reading Constable Chandler's spirited and largely verbatim report Pollard made a mental note that its author was a young man with considerable potential as a member of the CID, and on whom an eye should be kept. He went on to read the information on Mark Forbes gleaned from Woodshall on the outer margins of the Surrey stockbroker belt where he lived. The area was one of mainly youngish couples on the way up financially, and living well up to, if not beyond their incomes. There was a considerable mortgage on the Forbes house but they ran two classy cars and were much given to a wide variety of social activities. It had become obvious that the couple were drifting apart, and when Mrs Forbes left her husband for another man it caused little surprise. It was now believed that divorce proceedings were being set in motion on the grounds of the irretrievable breakdown of the marriage.

The reports seemed tiresomely irrelevant and Pollard pushed them impatiently to one side. With his elbows on his desk and his forehead resting on the palms of his hands he tried to clarify the situation to himself. Forbes had motive but no opportunity. Grimshaw's motive was not proven up to date, and although he might have got to the Durnycombe cliffs in time to carry out Paterson's murder he could not possibly have got himself back to the upper slopes of Twisterdown by about 11.30 that morning. A.N. Other then? Not the faintest suggestion of a third suspect had as yet emerged. There was, of course, one bit of the jigsaw which obstinately refused to fit in anywhere: the letter bomb, but it was a perfectly reasonable supposition that it had nothing whatever to do with Paterson's murder. As a matter of routine it was as well to find out if Grimshaw had a bicycle and could at any rate have got to Durnycombe in time to dispose of Paterson and the Caravette. At any rate it gave one the feeling of doing something. . . . Pollard's hand went out to the switch connecting him with the Yard's telephone switchboard but he finally withdrew it again. No point in seeming to hustle Minstow. He would go home for the night and ring early tomorrow morning. This time he asked the operator to put him through to his Wimbledon home. Within seconds one of his twins, Rose, aged eleven, was clearly and accurately giving the telephone number in the manner both she and her brother Andrew had been trained to do.

'Detective-Chief Superintendent Thomas Pollard speaking', he replied in a mock-official voice. 'Tell Mummy I'm just leaving the Yard for home, darling.'

He put down the receiver against a background of acclamation and a distant television programme.

After an evening of breathless outpourings by the twins, now in their first term at their respective senior schools, supper was cleared away and breakfast laid, and the children finally departed for bed. Pollard and Jane sank thankfully into their chairs in the sitting-room and sipped coffee in silence, Nox, the family's small

138

black cat, sat surveying them critically for a couple of minutes before opting for Jane's lap.

'What's the Nevinson situation like?' she asked presently.

'That,' Pollard replied, with a slight emphasis on the word, 'is fine. Charles was quite amazingly lucky, you know. If he hadn't turned to speak to Virginia just as he ripped open the jiffy bag he would probably have lost his sight. As it is, he's quite badly scarred on the left side of his neck, but they say plastic surgery can cope with that. As for Virginia, far from being reduced to a nervous wreck she strikes me as somehow having matured through the trauma of it all. It's difficult to explain. You know how she used to give the impression of still feeling insecure after the rotten time she'd had, even after her marriage. A bit too dependent on Charles, possibly. Having weathered this crisis she seems to have toughened up somehow.'

Jane made a sound of assenting comprehension.

'So it's this Paterson case that's biting you?' she asked after a silent interval.

'Yea. Could you stand it if I expound?'

'Of course. Go ahead.'

He had discussed all his important cases with her. On occasions she had expressed an indirect point of view which had sent him off on a new ultimately successful approach.

'I'll have to give you a certain amount of background,' he said. 'geographical and – well, sociological, for want of a better word. Minstow, as you may possibly remember from the Marleigh case is about six miles inland from a most spectacular coast. . . .'

When he eventually arrived at the depressing conclusion of complete bafflement she was silent for a full minute.

'Fascinating interweaving,' she said at last. 'I simply can't think how it can all be so clear to you when you haven't actually been over all the ground. The Coryport road and the garage and Durnycombe itself, for instance.' 'I've had maps innumerable, and Charles's case file was a text-book specimen of its kind,' he said, aware of the faintest trace of implied criticism in her comment. 'There just hasn't been time yet.'

'If the letter bomb *is* connected with the case,' Jane said meditatively, going off on another tack, 'surely the idea must have been to hold things up temporarily. Who wanted to hold what up?'

Pollard looked at her quickly.

'You know you could be on to something there. The obvious answer could be that Forbes wanted a chance to get to Lodwick first, to impress on the dim-witted Jean Naylor that she must on no account tell Nevinson that she had told him – Forbes, I mean – that Paterson was Linda Grimshaw's father. Forbes would be most reluctant to get involved in the enquiry into Paterson's death in any way because of the money. I must find out if either Super Lock or Charles himself told Forbes when he was due to go up to Lodwick to interview Mrs Ross. Not that it matters all that much, I suppose,' he concluded gloomily. 'Forbes is in the clear as far as Paterson's murder goes.'

Jane eyed her husband critically.

'What you need is some whisky and a good night's sleep,' she said.

Her recipe was effective. Pollard slept soundly through the night and woke to find his gloomy pessimism replaced by sheer dogged determination to find out who had carried out the Paterson murder and how. The job had been done by somebody, and therefore it must be possible by patient investigation to find out who this

140

somebody was. He put this point of view to Toye who agreed.

'Unless something's come in about a chap belting along the Minstow-Coryport road on a bike that Saturday morning,' he said. 'Not that even that would explain how Grimshaw got back up to the village place by half-past eleven, say.'

Nothing had come in, Superintendent Lock told them on their arrival at Minstow police station. With Coryport's co-operation there had been exhaustive enquiries over the past twenty-four hours.

'Bus drivers, commercial vehicles, people known to shop early on Saturday mornings in Coryport and Minstow – the whole bloody lot,' the Super elaborated. 'Except for a couple of dratted kids fooling about who oughtn't to have been on the road at all nobody seems to have noticed anyone on a bike.'

'There's worse to come, I'm afraid,' Pollard told him. 'Whatever Grimshaw was doing after he'd bought his chocolate at about 8.40, he was on that abandoned village site at 11.45.'

Superintendent Lock listened to a brief statement on the Penfolds and their evidence and swore vehemently.

'What's your next move?' he asked. 'Glad it's you to think one up and not me.'

'Back to Square One. The case file initially. We simply must have missed out on something.'

'Anything we can do, of course. Rope in Andrews if you want him. And if you want a reconstruction staged at Durnycombe or anywhere – ' He broke off to answer his telephone, and under cover of a conversation about a burglary Pollard and Toye removed themselves and made for their temporary office.

'One thing I'm quite clear about is that we're starting with a meal.' Pollard said. 'And not, repeat not, in the

141

canteen. We'll go back to the hotel and have a decent lunch.'

After halves of lager at the bar of the George and Dragon they progressed to the dining-room and ordered mixed grills. They were working steadily through these when Pollard suddenly broke the silence.

'If two minds are better than one,' he said, 'would you agree that four are better than two?'

Toye gave the matter his usual careful consideration and assented.

'It seems to me that there are three ways of going over the ground again. We can go through the file again, drive over the whole area from Little Underhill to Durny-combe, or get hold of two non-suspects who know the set-up and/or the people involved and see what comes out in discussion. I bet I know which one you'd put first.'

A grin spread over Toye's normally impassive face as he paused with a mushroom impaled on his fork.

'She only needs filling up,' he said. 'I had the tyres checked yesterday. Which two non-suspects had you got in mind?'

'Charles Nevinson himself, of course, for one, and Bill Appleton, the College Principal for the other. He has a personal knowledge of Paterson and Grimshaw, and Nevinson has met Forbes twice as well as interrogating Grimshaw. You'll be in on it too, naturally. . . . You can't possibly want a sweet or cheese after this grill. Let's have coffee and I'll ring Charles and Appleton while you get petrol put in. Leave room for taking on a gallon or two at Grey's Garage. It might help things on.'

On the road Pollard re-read Charles Nevinson's report on his interview with the Bulls. Their answers to his questions had been categorical and unembroidered. A tactful approach was called for to prevent their clamming up through irritation.

142

'You can size up the premises to see what sort of clientele the place has while I tackle the chaps,' he told Toye.

In the event the arrival of the Rover made a promising opening. Both the Bulls who were occupied with the engine of a muddy farm tractor disengaged themselves and came forward, contemplating the car with open admiration.

'Tidy job,' Jim Bull commented. 'What can us do for you gents?'

'Fill her up, please,' Pollard replied, 'but there's something else we want. A bit of help. We're the CID officers from Scotland Yard who've taken over the enquiry into the late Dr John Paterson's death.'

The Bulls stared at the official cards held out for their inspection.

'Us can't tell you nothin' more than us told the Minstow inspector. Him who 'ad the letter bomb sent to 'im, can us 'Arry?'

'Naw,' replied his son uncompromisingly.

'And a sergeant's been out here asking the same old questions all over again.'

'It's simply a matter of timing,' Pollard said. 'You see, Mr Bull, when we chaps from Scotland Yard have to take on a case in midstream, so to speak, we have to check up on the evidence that's handed over to us. It was just after 5 on the Friday evening, wasn't it, that Mr Forbes turned up with the windscreen of his Jag shattered? You can't have been any too pleased at getting landed with an urgent job right at the end of a day's work.'

Jim Bull thawed slightly in response to this sympathetic approach. It had been a bit of a bind, he admitted, but business wasn't all that good and you couldn't afford to turn away casual customers. Yes, just

143

after 5 when the gent pulled up. From this point Pollard led the conversation on to Harry's trip into Coryport to get a replacement screen, and the early start next morning to get the job done by 10. Both the Bulls contributed to the narrative, Harry adding the additional information that they'd got the windscreen fixed by quarter past nine. Conscious that Toye, while ostensibly following the discussion, was sizing up the garage and its contents, Pollard went on to the time at which the Caravette had driven past. Mr Forbes, he learnt, wanted to get away and had just got out his cheque book. . . . Every item in Charles Nevinson's report was corroborated down to his passing again on his return from Durnycombe to sort out the cameras.

'Just turned a quarter after ten, it 'ad,' Jim Bull said unhesitatingly. 'Take me oath in court, I would. We'd 'ad a cuppa and I was just sayin' to 'Arry that we'd bloody well better get a move on, the windscreen job 'aving thrown us all be'ind, see? Electric clock up there on the wall is never a minnit out, not unless there's a power cut, that is.'

Finally convinced, Pollard thanked him for his co-operation, exchanging a few remarks on the case while Harry put some petrol into the Rover under Toye's observant eye. This done, they moved off, heading for Durnycombe, Pollard noting the exact time of their departure. Toye was somewhat scathing about Grey's Garage. 'Mucky little place,' he said, 'cracked windows, dirty little wash basin and a filthy rag towel, and a great heap of junk: cartons, bins, broken glass and God only knows what, but they've got essential equipment for simple jobs, I'll grant them that.'

The Rover was faster on the road than Charles Nevinson's police car had been, but Toye's cautious negotiation of the rutted grassy track leading to the cliffs

144

compensated for this, and the journey once again took eight minutes.

They got out of the car and looked about them. The November afternoon was still and grey, the sky featureless apart from a faint luminosity to the south-west. In the slowly waning light the cliff top was a drab dun colour with occasional patches of evergreens now appearing almost black. From far below came the sound of waves breaking and the rattle of stones in the drag of ebbing water. A solitary seagull circled briefly overhead, gave a raucous cry and vanished. The most emphatic note of colour in the muted landscape was the dead white of waves breaking round the outermost isolated rock pinnacles far below in the grey sea. Pollard and Toye advanced with extreme caution and contemplated the clear traces of the Caravette's headlong descent over the edge of the cliff into the head of the cleft cut by Durnycombe Fall.

'Let's pack it in,' said Pollard, who was allergic to heights. 'The only point in coming out here was to check the timing.'

Toye complied, adding that the place gave him the willies.

Charles Nevinson had been enthusiastic over Pollard's suggestion of a meeting to discuss the case.

'I'm beginning to paw the ground,' he said. 'There's nothing really the matter with me now, and having to go to a bloody plastic surgery unit is the end. Still I can hardly expect Virginia to go round with a chap who looks as though he'd had the worst of a scrap for the rest of her life. Come along here tonight and we'll lay on drinks and snacks. Bill Appleton will play all right. He was in here last night and says life at the College is hell at the moment: gossip and rumours and nobody giving their minds to their jobs.'

Bill Appleton was obviously a very worried man. In response to Pollard's telephone call he replied that he would be only too glad to do anything he could to help, but was very doubtful of being able to contribute anything useful.

'I remember you very well, Chief Superintendent,' he said, 'over the Marleigh affair in the first place, and then at the Nevinsons' wedding. Half-past eight at their place, you said, didn't you?'

Over an early dinner at the George and Dragon Pollard began to feel increasingly worried at the lack of progress over the case, and to wonder if the meeting with Nevinson and Appleton could possibly contribute anything useful. If Grimshaw were the murderer in spite of this appearing to be a physical impossibility, his motive – the sheltering of Linda from learning that John Paterson was her father – could hardly be discussed in front of Appleton at this stage. He debated cancelling the fixture on some pretext or other, and then, quite suddenly, his mind went back to his conversation with Jane on the previous evening. It had evoked thoughts of that memorable telephone talk with her when he was right up against an apparent brick wall in his first case, and how she had said how important it surely must be to concentrate on the murderee who had, after all, sparked off his or her murder for some reason or other. . . .

He decided to let the evening go ahead as planned, and to begin with a detailed discussion of Paterson. This, at any rate, would amply justify Appleton's having been brought in.

The two cars arrived at the Nevinsons' house almost simultaneously, and Charles appeared at the front door.

'Come along in,' he said, leading the way into the

newly redecorated sitting-room. Four armchairs of a type inviting relaxation were drawn up to the fire, and a trolley with an array of bottles and glasses stood in the background. 'Virginia insists on our meeting in here. She says four grown men can't possibly squeeze into my minute study.'

As he was speaking Virginia came with with a tray of sandwiches and savouries. In the general exchange of greetings her increased confidence struck Pollard again.

'Really, we can't turn you out of your sitting-room,' he protested.

'Of course you must meet in here,' she said, putting the tray on the lower deck of the trolley. 'Four of you wouldn't be able to breathe in the study. I'd be in the kitchen anyway, because I *must* have a big table for working at the new curtains. So there I am, Charles, if more eats are wanted.'

She departed with a gay wave of her hand through the door held open by Toye. After her departure they settled down by the fire, Pollard with the case file on his knee. For a few minutes they talked generally. Finally there was a pause, he glanced round the semi-circle of chairs.

'Well, since I'm responsible for getting you all here I'd better justify myself,' he said. 'The plain truth is that we're at a dead end. I'll do a brief recap, if I may, starting from the sighting of the Caravette in the water at the bottom of Durnycombe Fall by that chap who was doing commercial photography from a helicopter on 26 October.'

Omitting only the information about Linda Grimshaw's parentage supplied by Grizel Ross, he outlined the successive stages of the enquiry into Paterson's death. Finally he gave it as his opinion that Paterson had told Grimshaw that he was not, after all,

147

retiring at the end of the academic year, and that this had been the last straw for Grimshaw and a credible motive for the murder.

'Mark Forbes's financial motive has always been credible,' he went on. 'So here we are with two suspects and two only, with motives to eliminate Paterson, neither of whom could possibly have done it. Bang up against a brick wall, in fact. Any comments. gentlemen?'

'Only,' Bill Appleton said after a pause, 'the purely personal one that, knowing Grimshaw as I do, I simply cannot see him as a cold-blooded deliberate murderer, even though Paterson had treated him like mud from the start. No one I have ever discussed it with has been able to understand why. . . . The general opinion has been that Paterson found him a convenient outlet for a sadistic streak. He undoubtedly had one. There have been one or two instances of students transferring to another department on the grounds that they couldn't get on with him.'

'He seems to have been a quite unusually unpleasant chap,' Pollard said. 'Could you fill in a bit more, Mr Appleton?'

'I've always found it difficult to understand why he had developed into such a bastard,' Bill Appleton said after a fairly lengthy pause. 'He apparently had a perfectly normal home and childhood. He came of good sound North Country stock. It was a textile manufacturing family which made a tidy bit of money over several generations, and he had inherited a life interest in the greater part of this as you know, of course. He went to a public school and took a good second class in the Natural Science Tripos at Cambridge, specialising in geology. Over the years he built up a modest reputation as a geologist, getting original work published. Physically he was remarkably fit for his age, and still doing quite demanding climbs in the Alps each summer vac. I've heard him boast that he'd never seen the inside of a hospital, and had every one of his own teeth and had never worn spectacles. Not bad for a chap of rising fifty-five, was it? He'd – '

Suddenly sensing a reaction from his listeners Bill Appleton looked up to find eyes rivetted on him.

'Then how do we account for the fact that a pair of spectacles was found in the pocket of a spare windcheater found in the Caravette?' Pollard asked. 'He'd taken a second lot of clothes and another pair of climbing boots as you'd expect.'

'They've all been dried off and are up at the station,' Nevinson said, 'and have been listed of course.'

'Were the spectacles in a case?' Pollard asked.

'If I could just take a look at the file, sir,' Toye said. 'Yes, they were,' he went on after a brief pause. 'One pair of horn-rimmed spectacles in a red case stamped with the maker's name: R.H. Woolmer, Opticians, 23 High Street, Minstow.'

Bill Appleton looked surprised.

'Now that strikes me as right out of character,' he said. 'Woolmer's is quite a modest local set-up though they've got properly qualified people, of course. I should have expected Paterson to go to a Harley Street man if that's where the top eye specialists congregate. As far as clothes and cars and general equipment for living went, only the best was good enough for John Paterson.'

'So you think the guff about never having worn spectacles was just projecting his personal image?' Pollard asked.

'Yes. That really seems the likely explanation. He'd probably got to the stage when he needed them for reading and writing by artificial light, and would have

149

been going to work on his notes in the Caravette after dark.'

'Well, we'll settle that by taking the specs along to R.H. Woolmer tomorrow morning. He'll be able to identify the prescription and say if they were Paterson's, or possibly a pair he'd picked up on the cliffs or somewhere and not bothered to hand in. . . . Could you go on with the sort of thing you were telling us, Mr Appleton?'

As Bill Appleton talked questions were raised about John Paterson's relations with members of the College staff other than Ronald Grimshaw, but no suggestion emerged of hostility violent enough to lead to his murder by a colleague. After a pause for drinks the discussion moved on to Grimshaw himself. As Pollard had expected doubts were expressed about the adequacy of his alleged motive. As Pollard listened he wondered what Bill Appleton's reaction would be to the possibility of Paterson having told Grimshaw –doubtless in the most offensive terms – of his own relationship to Linda.

'One thing in Grimshaw's favour as I see it,' Charles was saying, 'is the eternal time factor cropping up in this case. He'd got to get to Durnycombe between roughly twenty to nine and 9.45. I agree that it would be possible on that particular road given a decent bike. Paterson would have got to the cliffs at about five to ten, and Forbes, on your reckoning, Tom, at 10.06 approx. Grimshaw would not only have had to kill Paterson and send the Caravette over the edge, but also go to ground himself before Forbes turned up. There's not much cover and Forbes says he had a look in both directions along the cliff and there was nobody in sight. It's an incredibly tight fit, isn't it? And no bike's been found.'

It was agreed that Nevinson had a point there, but as Pollard reminded them there was also the problem of

150

Paterson's pre-fall injuries to solve. Appleton, an essentially honest thinker, commented on Grimshaw's apparent exhaustion when met by the Penfolds at the abandoned village some eleven miles away at about 11.30.

Finally they decided to call it a day.

Chapter Nine

On arriving at the premises of R.H. Woolmer, Optician, on the following morning, Pollard gave the receptionist his official card and asked her to take it in to Mr Woolmer himself.

'Please tell him,' he said, 'that I should be grateful if he could spare me a few minutes.'

The girl at the desk, a white-coated blonde over-weighted by an immense mop of tightly curled golden hair stared at the card, gaped at him and vanished precipitately through a door in the rear. A minute later she reappeared, eyed him incredulously and invited him to step this way.

Pollard was favourably impressed by the small elderly man who rose to meet him.

'Mr Woolmer?' he asked. 'Good morning. As I'm sure you know, I'm the CID officer in charge of the enquiry into the death of the late Dr Paterson of Minstow College, and this is Inspector Toye, my assistant. I think we have reached a point at which you could help us. We're anxious to know the name of the customer that you made this pair of spectacles for.'

He handed over the red case which was considerably the worse for several days' immersion in salt water. Mr

Woolmer took it with raised eyebrows, examined it carefully and extracted a pair of horn-rimmed spectacles. He held them up to his own eyes after polishing the lenses with a piece of wash leather.

'I think I can give you the information you want without much delay, sir,' he told Pollard. 'This is certainly our work of about two or three years back. There's a fashion in spectacles like in everything else these days, and this pair would look a bit out of date now, for our younger customers anyhow. They were made up on a National Health prescription for someone – almost certainly a man – with a slight degree of short sightedness. I may add,' he went on, giving Pollard a shrewd glance, 'that Dr Paterson was never a customer of ours. Say an hour for testing the lenses accurately and tracking down the prescription in our records. Would you care to take a seat in the waiting area?'

'Let's take a stroll around,' Pollard said, turning to Toye. 'We'll be back at half-past ten then, Mr Woolmer, and many thanks.'

It was a pale-blue misty morning with faint sunlight. They made for the Cathedral and sat down on a bench in the Close.

'Well, they weren't Paterson's specs that he wouldn't admit to needing,' Toye said. 'Do you think there's anything in it for us?'

'Probably not,' Pollard replied. 'At first it looked like a possible lead. You grab at any possible lead when a case is as stuck as this one is, but the explanation's more likely to be nothing whatever to do with Paterson's murder. A windcheater's the sort of thing he'd wear when he was out geologising, and he probably had several.. He could quite well have picked up the case which someone had dropped and meant to hand it in to

153

Woolmer and forgot about it, or just couldn't be bothered. . . . Where do we go from here, then? I wish these Minstow people wouldn't go in for fatal car crashes and letter bombs and then pass the buck to the Yard. It's anything but easy to take over a case in midstream. I haven't yet interviewed either Forbes or Grimshaw, let alone the supporting cast such as Forbes's solicitor and Mrs Grimshaw.'

After discussion it was agreed that on returning to the police station Pollard should ring Grimshaw, playing it cool and agreeing to an appointment at the time most convenient to him. When this had been fixed up the next step had better be contacting Forbes and making a similar arrangement with him.

'He may be out on a job and take a bit of tracking down,' Pollard said. 'We'll suggest coming up to London, of course. With any luck we might get a spot of home life on the side. Listen . . . matins are just starting from the sound of it. Go inside and enjoy the music for quarter of an hour while I contemplate the architecture from outside. Then we'll go back to Woolmers.'

They were shown straight into Mr Woolmer's office on arrival and Pollard caught sight of the red spectacle case on his desk, acting as a paperweight to a short typewritten statement.

'There was no problem, gentlemen, I'm glad to say,' they were told. 'I traced the prescription with very little difficulty. These spectacles were made for a Mr Ronald Grimshaw just two years ago. His vision defect was a very minor degree of short-sightedness, and there's a note that he wanted glasses for driving, not day-to-day use. His address is 3, Rosemary Close, Minstow, if you want to get in touch with him. I've made a short summary of these facts for you.'

Pollard thanked Mr Woolmer and apologised for

having taken up his time. Then, disregarding the obvious interest in the optician's face, managed to escape before any awkward questions could be asked. Outside, the streets were crowded with the morning's shoppers and conversation was impracticable. They made their way back to the police station and the seclusion of their temporary office. Toye looked across the table, sensed an undercurrent of excitement in Pollard, and decided to play what he called his damping-down role.

'Could be,' he suggested, 'that Paterson knew well enough they were Grimshaw's glasses and hung on to 'em out of devilment.'

'There's something else it could be,' Pollard replied, folding his arms and leaning back in his chair. 'It hit me just as we were coming along. Here it is, old son, for you to knock down: the driver of the Caravette that morning wasn't Paterson. It was Grimshaw togged up as Paterson.'

Toye, momentarily speechless, sat staring at him.

'Paterson,' Pollard went on in a conversational tone which imperfectly concealed his excitement, 'made the journey too, of course. As a stiff, conveniently hidden from view in the covered part of the Caravette. You remember, don't you, that the Yard medicos and forensic scientists thought that the knock on the head that did for him had happened not less than two hours before he went down the Durnycombe Cliff and into the water? Of course it's the sort of thing Counsel for the Defence could argue about for hours in court, but it's our blokes' considered opinion.'

'But,' Toye said on regaining the power of speech, 'they must both have been in it. Forbes *and* Grimshaw. That postman saw the Caravette and the Mini coming down the lane from Loyes Cottage together that Saturday morning.'

'This is it. Why in the name of all that's holy didn't it dawn on us before? It was a two-man job. At some time – probably in the last year or two – Forbes decided to liquidate Paterson in order to get his hands on the family money. Paterson was a hale and hearty type who could easily have hung on into his eighties. The problem was when and how to do the job. I think Forbes saw a possible opportunity coming up when he knew Iremongers would be sending him down to the Minstow area to vet a bunch of properties in the week beginning 16 October. He rang Paterson and asked to be put up for the night of the 19th. Paterson would have emphasised that he was starting off first thing on the Saturday morning to do some fieldwork at Durnycombe, camping in the Caravette. To Forbes what appeared to be a heaven-sent chance presented itself. He saw the possibility of staging a breakdown of his car on the Coryport road and asking to be put up at Loyes Cottage for the night of the 20th, too. More important, he also saw the value of an accomplice to provide himself with a cast-iron alibi. And thanks to Jean Naylor he was in a position to blackmail Grimshaw with the threat of telling Linda that the man who had made her husband's life sheer hell was her father.'

'Forbes couldn't possibly have known that Linda Grimshaw was going to be away that Friday and Saturday,' Toye objected stoutly. 'Grimshaw couldn't have come in on the scheme if she'd been around.'

'Hold it!' Pollard said. 'Where's the file? Turn up the record of our Lodwick interviews.'

They hunted through the accumulation of papers and sat poring over the transcript of the conversation with Jean Naylor.

'The dates tie up,' Pollard said. 'Forbes learnt about Paterson being Linda's father on his visit to Lodwick in

156

July, didn't he? And about her commitment to her friend's wedding.'

'But how could Forbes have known for sure that Grimshaw would be prepared to connive at murder?' Toye asked, adhering firmly to his chosen role of devil's advocate.

'My guess is,' Pollard replied, 'that Forbes somehow contacted Grimshaw after he himself had killed Paterson or had decided to kill him early on the Saturday morning, and blackmailed him into helping to get rid of the body by staging the accident at Durnycombe. It wasn't the same thing as actually conniving at murder.'

'All right, I'll buy that,' Toye said rather reluctantly, after a pause. 'But Grimshaw was buying chocolate at that shop near his home at about 8.40 that Saturday morning. How did he get to Loyes Cottage in time to tog up in Paterson's windcheater and whatever, and start off driving the Caravette by just after 9?'

'I'm surprised at a chap with a car fixation like yours being unable to work that one out,' Pollard said with a grin. 'Look at the town plan of Minstow. Forbes would have been waiting on the Hill Road to pick him up and run him to Loyes Cottage in a matter of minutes.'

'But think of the risk – I'd go beyond that and say the probability of being spotted. I'll grant you there wouldn't be a lot of traffic on that road at that time of day, but a posh Jag! – '

He broke off abruptly.

'Got it, old man?' Pollard asked. 'The Jag was sitting pretty at Grey's Garage, wasn't it? Forbes would have been driving the old Mini he'd hired from the Bulls.'

Toye conceded the point, and that the old Mini was more unremarkable.

'And Forbes picked him up in his Jag at Durny-combe,' he went on, 'when he'd driven over there on the

157

muddled camera racket. And Grimshaw lay on the floor at the back?'

'That's how I think they worked it. Forbes would have pulled into an offside layby on the London road after handing in the camera to Mrs Dredge, and told Grimshaw to get out during a lull in the traffic and shin up the side of Twisterdown to the village site. Like the side of the house, isn't it? No wonder the Penfolds thought he looked all in and didn't seem to have got much work done.'

After another silence Toye asked if there was any prospect of bringing a charge on what they had got.

'No,' Pollard said reluctantly. 'The AC would merely congratulate me on an imaginative reconstruction unsupported by what he calls solid concrete evidence. Lab stuff. Microscope stuff. Actual witnesses of A slogging B over the head. Even these glasses aren't in that category,' he went on, taking up the red case and extracting the contents. 'As we agreed, Paterson could have found them, knew they were Grimshaw's and hung on to them for the hell of it.'

As he spoke he tried the pair on and gazed round the room, remarking that it was amazing how two bits of glass could sharpen your vision. Suddenly he stiffened, took the glasses off and put them down slowly and deliberately on the table.

'If you wanted to smash you car's windscreen while you were on the road and make it look like an accident from a flying stone how would you set about it?' he asked.

Startled, Toye considered the matter.

'I'd pull into a lane, out of sight of passing traffic, get out and preferably find a not too large stone and land the glass a pretty hefty whack coming upwards, if you get me. Then I'd get into the car and protect my hand with

158

something and push the shattered bits outwards so that I could see to drive, and edge out again.'

Pollard was unconsciously sitting bolt upright.

'You said there was glass, didn't you, in that pile of junk at the back of Grey's Garage? Anything that could have been a Jag's windscreen?'

'Yes.'

Pollard was on his feet.

'Come on. Pick up some sandwiches in the canteen, will you? We may be some time. . . .'

At Grey's Garage a pair of legs in grimy jeans protruded from under a Ford Cortina. As Pollard and Toye got out of the Rover Jim Bull emerged from a roughly partitioned-off cubicle which apparently served as an office. At the sight of them he stopped in his tracks.

'God A'mighty, not the cops again!' he exclaimed. ''Twill be the fourth bleedin' time, and the same bleedin' questions over an' over again.'

'Not this time, Mr Bull,' Pollard told him. 'Quite a different question. When you and your son put a new windscreen into Mr Forbes's Jaguar what did you do with the old one?'

Harry Bull extricated himself from under the Cortina and joined his father.

'Why, 'twas all to bits,' he said. 'Us chucked 'em on the scrap 'eap.' He gestured in the direction of the mound of debris which had so affronted Toye, flicked on a second bar of strip lighting and led the way towards it. Pieces of glass were visible in the mêlée of torn cartons, discarded empty containers, old sacks and unidentifiable litter.

'Whereabouts in the screen was the hole that Mr Forbes smashed through after it was shattered?' Toye asked. 'In the centre?'

'More on the offside.' Jim Bull eyed Pollard and Toye with signs of mounting truculence. ''Ere, what's all this in aid of? Us did the job, and that's all we knows about it.'

'It's in aid, Mr Bull, of finding out who murdered Dr Paterson,' Pollard told him, 'and we are almost certain that the shattered windscreen comes into it. We want your help in collecting up as many of the pieces as we can. We shall need to take them up to Scotland Yard, to the technicians who work in our laboratories. And it's most important that the press and the TV chaps don't get on to this. Can we count on you to choke them off if they come nosing round, and to keep the whole thing under your hats at home and in the pub?'

The Bulls stared at him.

'Seems cockeyed to me,' Jim said at last, 'but I reckon chaps o' your rank knows what 'ems about. Us'll keep mum till it all comes out in the papers, won't us, 'Arry? 'Ere,' he went on as Toye advanced on the rubbish heap. 'Best to let us grub in this muck, seein' we're in our workin' clothes.'

About a third of the Jaguar's windscreen was recovered unsplintered in one piece, wrapped in an old sack and put aside. A considerable number of fragments of mainly splintered glass and of various sizes were collected in a plastic bag. Finally, after thanking the Bulls with a genuineness which he felt got across to them, Pollard and Toye got into the Rover and drove off in the direction of Coryport, aware of being followed by a baffled but curious gaze.

'So far, so good,' Pollard said. 'Keep your eyes skinned now for the sort of track leading off the road that no normal wheeled traffic would use. You do the offside and I'll concentrate on the near one. There's the Durnycombe lane, of course, but you could never be

160

sure somebody mightn't turn up, either heading for the cliffs or coming away.'

They drove for a couple of miles without passing any other little-used turning. Suddenly they approached an ancient five-barred wooden gate standing wide open and apparently leading into a field of rough grass and clumps of bracken.

'Turn in after hesitating a bit,' Pollard. 'Anyone coming along in a car will think we've got a picnic lunch on board.'

Toye successfully, if reluctantly, manoeuvred the car over bumpy ground into the empty field and bore left under cover of a thick hedge. They got out and began to scrutinise the surface. A few yards further on the signs of vegetation flattened by tyres came to an end, and fragments of broken glass among the tangle of the plant cover sent up sharp points of reflected light.

In the late afternoon a hastily convened conference took place at Minstow police station, attended by Major Waller, Superintendent Lock, Pollard, Toye, and at Pollard's special request, a still bandaged Charles Nevinson.

'After all,' he had argued with Lock, 'it's really his case, and by God he put in some good groundwork for us to build on.'

Pollard's précis of the facts which had convinced him that Forbes had murdered his uncle, and that Grimshaw had been blackmailed into helping with the disposal of the body was listened to in almost complete silence and followed by a chorus of congratulation.

'It's really Appleton who provided the breakthrough,' Pollard said, 'by chancing to mention that Paterson habitually bragged about never having worn glasses. But don't let's get carried away. We're by no means home and dry. The windscreen's got to be reconstructed as far as possible and the glass confirmed by the Jag people as the type used in that particular model. And we've no tangible proof yet that Grimshaw travelled from Durnycombe to some point on the London road at the foot of Twisterdown, probably on the floor or under rugs on the back seat. Grimshaw may come clean, of course, if the AC gives the go-ahead for pulling in Forbes on what we've got, and if this happens our forensic chaps can get going on the Jag.'

'Hairs?' queried Nevinson. 'Grimshaw's, on the floor at the back?'

'Exactly. They have a way of sticking to things and escaping notice, fortunately for the likes of us.'

Half an hour later the Scotland Yard Rover was London bound with Pollard, Toye and the broken remains of the windscreen on board. These latter were handed over to one of the Yard's labs.

'Nice little job for you here,' Pollard told the senior technician. 'Kids' stuff. Just reassemble the jigsaw, that's all. You'll find quite a few bits missing roughly right of centre, though. I'll look in tomorrow morning and see how you're getting on.' A few ribald remarks were exchanged before he left to leave a brief report with his AC's secretary and started for home.

After supper, when at last the twins had been got off to bed, Jane Pollard contemplated her husband lying back in his favourite chair with closed eyes. He was dog-tired, she thought. All the endless chases from one end of the country to the other, even if Toye was a marvellous driver. She wondered what it would be like to have a nine-to-five husband. . . .

He opened his eyes and looked at her in amusement.

'I was not, repeat not, asleep,' he said. 'Sometimes I

sits and thinks and sometimes I just sits. This time I was sitting and thinking. Do you remember the Meldon School case back in the Dark Ages?'

'Heavens! Of course I do. Your first big case. The nervous strain nearly killed me. Why?'

'It was a remark of yours that put me on the right track just when everything seemed deadlocked. I rang you from a callbox to keep my spirits up, and you said that it seemed to you that the clue to a murder case really lay in the victim. Personality, circumstances and so on. Well, when I was here the other evening and we were talking over this Durnycombe business that remark came back to me, and seems to have hovered on the surface of my subconscious mind. Anyway, on the evening of the following day I was inspired to get Charles and Bill Appleton, the Principal of Minstow College, to come along and have a sort of talk-in. I said I wanted to discuss Paterson. And Appleton who knew him best, of course, got going and said how amazingly fit the chap was, and how he swaggered about it. Said he'd never seen the inside of a hospital or worn a pair of spectacles. The word spectacles turned out to be a catalyst . . . '

'Don't bother to ask if I can take a re-cap up to date,' Jane said, 'I simply can't wait . . . '

During the two days needed to reassemble the windscreen a sample of the glass was sent to the makers of the car. In their turn they submitted it to their suppliers who confirmed that it was the type used for models of the date owned by Mark Forbes.

'This should do the trick as far as the AC goes,' Pollard remarked to Toye as he attached the manufacturers' report to his own detailed statement on the enquiry into John Paterson's murder.

The AC showed himself sufficiently interested to visit the laboratory and inspect the finished version of what had become popularly known as Pollard's Jigsaw. While waiting until the late afternoon to be summoned to discuss what action should be taken in the light of the accumulated evidence, Pollard forced himself to face squarely his growing uneasiness about the outcome of charging both Forbes and Grimshaw. It was something of a relief when he was called to the AC's office. He found his Chief sitting at his desk with the file of the enquiry in front of him.

'Interesting case as usual,' the AC commented sardonically. 'You're right about holding our hand for the moment, though. Obviously unless we can prove Grimshaw's involvement or get him to admit it, if Forbes were brought to trial on the murder charge he'd get off on the alibi provided by those garage chaps. You argue that Grimshaw will deny involvement in order to conceal from his wife the grounds on which Forbes was blackmailing him into helping in the disposal of the body. Right. Well then, as I see no prospect of getting Grimshaw to come clean we've somehow got to prove that he impersonated Paterson, drove the Caravette over the cliff with the body in it, was picked up by Forbes on the alleged camera changing trip to Durnycombe a few minutes later, and was dropped off somewhere at the bottom of that hill –Twisterdown, it is called, isn't it? – on the Minstow-London road. I agree with that up-and-coming young chap Nevinson that if Grimshaw travelled in Forbes's car on the floor at the back or on the back seat there'd almost certainly be traces of hair or fingerprints. Well, we've got to get hold of that car and get our forensics to go over it with a toothcomb, and without Forbes cottoning on. Get Toye to think out something. He's a car buff if ever there was one. . . . What's in your mind, Pollard, for God's sake?'

'Wouldn't the best way out be to let Mrs Grimshaw know the truth about herself, sir? Her husband could then plead that he acted under the duress of blackmail and would get a much lighter sentence, while Forbes would be convicted of wilful murder with blackmail thrown in. Justice done, and seen to be done, in fact.'

Pollard, from long experience of his AC, detected a gleam of approval in the stony stare to which he was subjected.

'And who do you suggest should break the truth to the unfortunate woman? Yourself?'

'No, sir. Mrs Grizel Ross who is her great-aunt on her father's side. You'll have gathered something of her quality and experience in public life from Toye's verbatim record of my conversation with her at Lodwick. And it's a family affair, come to that.'

'Now look here, Pollard,' the AC replied, switching on to a familiar reaction to any somewhat unconventional suggestion from a member of his department. 'Kindly understand one thing. I cannot have this case dragging on indefinitely. I'm not saying there aren't some possibilities in this suggestion of yours, but a murder is on our hands and Forbes and Grimshaw are both involved, and I want them pulled in as soon as possible and charged.'

'Mrs Ross isn't the sort to let the grass grow under her feet, sir. If I started first thing tomorrow I could be in Lodwick by lunch time and see her in the afternoon. If you approve I'll ring her right away and make an appointment. And if I share the driving with Toye we could be back tomorrow night.'

There was a short pregnant pause.

'Get on with it then,' the AC barked. 'Find somebody to take on the job of investigating Forbes's car, though. Concrete definite evidence is what we want.'

165

Escaping thankfully to his own office Pollard contacted the switchboard, gave them Grizel Ross's telephone number and asked for a priority call to be put through.

Less than twenty-four hours later Pollard and Toye were sitting in Grizel Ross's drawing-room, facing her across the hearth. As he talked it flashed through Pollard's mind that she was an even more impressive personality in daylight. Her still bright, clear and acutely appraising eyes, perhaps. . . .

'Well, I think that's a fair statement of the present position, Mrs Ross,' he concluded.

She remained silent for almost a minute.

'I frankly disliked my late nephew, John Paterson, but he had a right to live,' she said at last. 'My great-nephew Mark Forbes has, too, in my opinion. I am not in favour of capital punishment, and if we still had the death penalty I shouldn't have felt able to do what you suggest: tell Mrs Grimshaw that John was her father and so make it unnecessary for her husband to conceal the fact that he was blackmailed into the disposing of his body. Once Mr Grimshaw admits having impersonated John, Mark's carefully worked-out alibis collapse, don't they? . . . I shall go down to Minstow, see Linda Grimshaw and make suitable arrangements for her immediate future, poor child. Mr Grimshaw will presumably be charged with being an accessory to the murder? What sentence is he likely to get?'

'It's difficult to say at this stage, Mrs Ross,' Pollard replied. 'His defence will plead extenuating circumstances on the grounds of his being blackmailed in a particularly unpleasant way, but he has committed a serious offence in disposing of Dr Paterson's body with the intent of misleading the police. I should expect him to get a short term of imprisonment. Just possibly a suspended sentence.'

'He will lose his present post, of course,' Grizel Ross said thoughtfully. 'Naturally I shall concern myself with his future as well as with my great-niece's. Shall we now briefly discuss immediate plans for my visit to Minstow?'

Late though it was when they arrived back in London Pollard called in at the Yard. A message from his secretary was on his desk: the AC wished to see him at 11 o'clock the next morning. Pollard's eyebrows went up. Must be feeling a bit steamed up over the case, he reflected. By rights he'd be off duty tomorrow. Going down in the lift he admitted that it had been a long day and braced himself for the final effort of driving home to Wimbledon.

As he had expected the interview on the following morning began with protests about the delay involved in bringing Mrs Ross into the case. Somewhat mollified by hearing that she was travelling down to Minstow on Monday and would pay the vital visit to Linda Grimshaw on Tuesday morning, the AC demanded details of Pollard's own proposed programme.

'I propose to pull in Forbes before he leaves his home on Tuesday morning, sir, and take him straight down to Minstow. By the time we get there Mrs Ross will have told Linda Grimshaw that Paterson was her father, and when Grimshaw comes home at lunch time he'll be faced with the fact that there's no longer any need to deny having helped Forbes to dispose of Paterson. We shall arrest him on a charge of conspiring with another to commit murder, and get him a solicitor who will obviously persuade him to plead guilty under the duress of blackmail by Forbes.'

'Neat,' the AC conceded, 'but it's a cock-eyed business. You've never set eyes on either of the suspects.'

'I've been briefed on them *ad nauseam* by Nevinson,

167

Lock, Appleton and Mrs Ross, sir. There was a studio photograph of Grimshaw in the sitting-room of their house. I memorised it while his wife was making me a cup of coffee. Chandler snitched a colour brochure of the Iremonger set-up when he went to pump Forbes's secretary about him. I feel I'm pretty well clued up on both.

The AC sniffed.

'It's also worth bearing in mind that Forbes is a bloody clever type to have planned this job, and bloody dangerous, too. Lock should never have let on that he was sending Nevinson up to see Mrs Ross. Forbes saw the potential danger to himself at once. Under questioning the Naylor girl would let on that she'd told him about Paterson being Mrs Grimshaw's father and so given him the means of blackmailing Grimshaw into helping with the murder. So he decided to knock out Nevinson, at any rate temporarily, and bank on a hold-up before anyone could be found to go in his place. No doubt he intended to shut Naylor's mouth by proposing to her. Or alternatively by scaring the living daylights out of her. Last night after work was his first chance of getting at her. He wouldn't want to ask for yet another day off from Iremonger's with the adjourned inquest next week. Do you want to put an application for guns? You'll take Toye, of course, and a third?'

Pollard considered.

'I'd prefer not, sir. Grimshaw wouldn't know what to do with one, I'm perfectly convinced, and equally convinced that Forbes's tactics will be to express outrage and demand a solicitor. You see, until we tumbled to the impersonation racket he had the alibi provided by the Bulls. He won't know that the whole thing has come unstuck.'

The AC unexpectedly grinned.

'Go ahead then. Only don't find that Forbes reacts by plugging you and making a dash for it. We're short of experienced blokes just now.'

Detective-Sergeant Wells who had visited Woodshall and gathered information about the Forbes ménage, was the obvious choice for the third man stipulated by the AC. He had the additional advantage of being an ex-commando just in case Forbes resisted arrest. His talents did not include artistic ability, but with encouragement from Pollard and Toye he produced a rough sketch-plan of the house and garage which was approached by a short drive leading from a relatively quiet road on the outskirts of the village. Reference to Detective-Constable Chandler's report on his conversation with Forbes's secretary at Iremonger Properties' head office produced the information that he was never known to be late in arriving at 9 o'clock, zero hour for his grade.

Toye, after a careful study of road maps, announced that take-off time on Tuesday morning had better be 6 a.m. He undertook to be in touch with the AA about road and weather conditions in case an earlier start was advisable. In the event no road hazards were reported and the Rover slipped across Westminster Bridge as Big Ben sonorously announced the hour.

The tension which always built up immediately before an arrest expressed itself in a largely silent drive. Against a background awareness of the sunrise beauty of a calm autumn morning Pollard's mind reviewed the chain of logical reasoning which had led to the action ahead. At intervals the awareness of being in command and responsible for the safety of Toye and Wells asserted itself uncomfortably. Should all three of them

169

have been armed after all? Then, after a few minutes of agonising self-doubt, logical reasoning based on evidence would reassert itself. Forbes, supremely confident in his time-factor alibi, would play it cool. It must have given him an unpleasant jolt to find that in spite of the delaying tactics of the letter bomb the police had got to Lodwick ahead of him, but Jean Naylor, infatuated with him, would surely have flatly denied having done what he seemed so anxious about: admitting to them that she had told him that Paterson was Linda Grimshaw's father. In her limited way she must have wondered why it mattered. . . .

Toye broke into his thoughts by announcing that they would be at Woodshall in ten minutes. Unconsciously he shifted his position and braced himself.

They took a route which avoided the centre of the village, and under Wells's direction drew up half a dozen yards beyond the drive entrance to Mark Forbes's house. Pollard got out with him to make a recce. Just inside the gate which was propped open the drive made a slight curve. They advanced cautiously to a point at which they could see the house. A single ground-floor window was a rectangle of strong light. They pressed against some shrubs as a car drove past along the road.

'Having his breakfast,' Wells said quietly. 'That's the kitchen. Garage door's shut. We can't fail to hear him start.'

Their tactic was simplicity itself. Very quietly they closed and latched the drive gate and returned to the car ostensibly immersed in a discussion of business papers, but there was little passing traffic as yet. Inevitably tension mounted as the light strengthened, etching in the main features of the landscape.

At last the door slammed and steps were audible. Moments later a strident grinding sound indicated the swinging up of the garage door. A car door slammed and an engine started up. Tyres crunched on gravel with increasing velocity. At the sight of the closed gate the driver jammed on his brakes and got out, cursing audibly. Turning to get into the car again he almost collided with the three men who had silently emerged from shrubs bordering the drive.

'I am Detective-Chief Superintendent Pollard of New Scotland Yard,' Pollard informed him, 'and I arrest you, Mark Hamish Forbes, on a charge of unlawfully killing John Hamish Paterson on the twenty-first of October this year.'

Toye and Wells closed in unobtrusively, but Mark Forbes made no attempt to move. Looking at the reddish-brown hair and eyebrows, the blunt features and calculating steel-grey eyes of the Iremonger Properties brochure photograph Pollard waited for the expected response.

'Make a bloody fool of yourself if you like,' he was told. 'My solicitor will give you every assistance. Even those clods at Minstow know that it was a sheer physical impossibility for me to have murdered my uncle.'

'This way, sir, if you please.' Toye and Wells each took a firm grip of one of his arms and impelled him towards the Rover in the road outside. A boy on a newspaper round stared, open mouthed.

'My God, you'll regret this,' Pollard was told with confident relish.

At mid-morning Linda Grimshaw went to her front door in response to the melodic chimes of its bell. Expecting to see a neighbour on the doorstep she was taken aback by being confronted by a total stranger, a tall elderly woman with white hair wearing an old-fashioned but obviously

171

costly black fur coat.

'Mrs Grimshaw?' the caller enquired in what Linda instantly classified as a genuine U voice, rather deep and with a slight North Country inflexion. Her previous secretarial training came to her rescue.

'Yes,' she replied, smiling politely. 'I'm Mrs Grimshaw. Can I help you?'

'You can,' she was told, 'but may I come in and sit down? I find standing about rather tiring these days.'

'But of course. Please do. Come into the lounge.' Speaking rather disconnectedly from a sense of having failed to show the social poise she aspired to, Linda led the way and pulled forward a comfortable chair. 'May I make you a cup of coffee?'

'No thank you, my dear. I breakfasted much later than usual this morning. I came down to Minstow from my home in Lodwick yesterday. Quite a long journey.'

Feeling increasingly puzzled by her visitor, Linda grasped at a far-distant memory of a coach outing organised as a holiday treat in her Harringtons days.

'Yes, it must have been,' she said. 'Lodwick's in Northshire, isn't it?'

'Quite right, my dear, it is. How do you come to know that? It's quite a small place.'

Linda flushed faintly.

'Oh, I was at boarding school in the next county, so I must have heard about it.'

'I see. Well, now you know where I come from I had better introduce myself. I'm Mrs Grizel Ross and your great-aunt.'

In her sheer astonishment Linda reacted spontaneously.

'You can't be. I'm – I'm . . .'

'Illegitimate,' Grizel Ross supplied briskly. 'I know. Your father was my nephew.'

172

The flash of delight that lit up Linda's face died away with equal suddenness.

'You said "was" your nephew. Has he died?'

'He has,' Grizel Ross replied, looking at her keenly. 'He died on the twenty-first of October this year. I think that date means something to you, doesn't it, Linda?'

For several moments there was complete silence. Linda sat immobilised by an unformulated dread. Suddenly an appalling possibility took shape in her mind.

'You don't mean?' she whispered, going very white. 'You can't . . .

'I do, my dear. Now you are going to listen to me. We've both got Paterson blood in our veins. It was my maiden name, you see. Patersons have in varying degrees exceptional determination. For better or worse, of course. Your father, John Paterson, I regret to say, expressed his by crass selfishness and trampling underfoot anybody who hadn't the mental make-up to stand up to him. People such as your husband. You are going to use your own quota to rebuild your husband's life. With my assistance, of course.'

'Rebuild Ron's life?' Linda momentarily distracted from the shock she had received stared at her. 'You mean help him show a bit more push and drive now that he'll be practically certain to get the Department?'

'The rebuilding's going to involve a lot more than that, you know. That's where your own Paterson determination must come in. You see, I have a great-nephew called Mark Forbes, whose mother was your father's sister. His sights were on the power that making money on a really big scale brings. Only, if you're going to get to the top in that world you need to spend money to start with. Your father had what is called a life interest in the Paterson money and it

173

wouldn't come to Mark until John's death. So he planned John's murder. It was a very ingenious plan but he needed a helper. By sheer misfortune he found out that John was your father, and threatened to tell you unless your husband agreed to be that helper. It was his job to drive the Caravette over the cliff with your father's dead body inside. Mark Forbes had killed him before they left Loyes Cottage, you see.'

Linda sat frozen in rigidity. At last she swallowed and managed to speak.

'Have the police found out about Ron helping?'

'Yes, they have,' Grizel Ross said gently.

'Will he be sent to prison?'

'Probably, but speaking as someone who has been a JP for many years, I do not think he would get a long sentence. He has been a blackmailer's victim, you see.'

Another silence fell.

'And Ron made himself do such an awful thing just so that I need never know that John Paterson who'd bullied and insulted him for years – was – my –father. . . . Where is Ron? I want him. Now.' She sat twisting her hands together in her tension.

Grizel Ross looked at her thoughtfully.

'That remark you made just now about getting your husband to show more push and drive was revealing,' she said with apparently irrelevance. 'You're the stronger partner, I take it?'

'I'm more of a fighter. I've had to be. Being illegitimate and coming from an orphanage doesn't help, even these days. Ron's always been afraid he'd lose his job if he stood up to – to John Paterson. I've often said to him I wished he'd go and tell the Principal what he had to put up with and walk out. I'd have gone to work as a daily help to keep us. . . . I *must* go to him. Will the police take him away?'

174

Grizel Ross glanced at the clock on the mantelpiece. 'At this moment he is almost certainly with Detective-Chief Superintendent Pollard of Scotland Yard who came to take over the case after Inspector Nevinson had been sent that letter bomb, almost certainly by Mark. You will be allowed to see him and take him anything he wants later today. Tomorrow he will come up before the magistrates and his solicitor will apply for his release on bail. I shall, of course, offer to be his surety . . .'

Grizel Ross was right in surmising that Ron Grimshaw was with Pollard, but the circumstances would have surprised her. At the end of the second lecture period of the morning he had returned as usual to his room for a cup of coffee. Anne Brothers appeared with it on a small tray.

'Somebody's been arrested on a charge of murdering Dr Paterson,' she remarked unemotionally, setting it down on his desk. 'It was the first item on the news bulletin a few minutes ago, they said in the pantry. Somebody called Forbes. Would you like to go on with your letters when you've had your coffee?'

Ron Grimshaw felt himself go deadly cold.

'I'll buzz you when I'm ready to start,' he heard his voice saying. 'There's something I must see to first.'

Pressed for time because of his new responsibilities he now always drove to the College from Rosemary Close. Going down in the lift he hurried to the car park and got into his car. As he reached the entrance he swerved to pass a black Rover with a London registration number and three men on board, and failed to notice the swift reaction of one of them.

'Sir!' Sergeant Andrews had exclaimed. 'The chap in that Cortina's Grimshaw.'

175

Toye reacted instantly by making a swift turn inside the car park.

'Tail him,' Pollard said tersely. 'He's making for the Coryport road.'

The mid-morning traffic was heavy. For a full minute they lost sight of the Cortina. Then Toye contrived to get past a bus and it came in view again.

'Edge up when you get a chance,' Pollard told him. 'He won't know the car, but he's seen you before, Andrews. Keep your head down.'

After years of working closely with Pollard, Toye had become adept at reading his mind.

'Think he's heading for Durnycombe?' he asked.

'For the bottom of bloody Durnycombe Fall, I'm afraid,' Pollard said grimly. 'If it's humanly possible we've got to stop him.'

Beyond Grey's Garage Toye began to reduce the distance between the two cars, risking a dangerous overtake and being hooted at by an indignant driver. Suddenly Grimshaw slightly reduced speed and swerved violently left into the Durnycombe Lane with the Rover now only a few yards behind him. Toye astonished Pollard by his vocabulary as the cherished Rover jolted and lurched over the rutted stony surface of the lane.

'Stop him,' Pollard said authoritatively as they approached its end, 'but not at the risk of going over ourselves. That's an order.'

As the Cortina approached the open area at the top of the cliffs, Grimshaw, a less-experienced driver than Toye, hesitated fractionally. With a sudden rush of speed Toye swept the Rover round to the space in front of it, braking a few inches from its radiator. Grimshaw was out a fraction of a second ahead of Pollard, running for the cliff. Here, where the Caravette had torn up the ground he tripped, stumbled and vanished over the

176

edge. Sick with horror Pollard arrived to look down and saw him struggling to free himself from the mass of brambles which were hanging half-wrenched up and loose.

'Keep still, you bloody fool,' he heard himself shout. 'Linda knows Paterson was her father.'

The struggles stopped. Their eyes met. Grimshaw swallowed and passed his tongue over his lips.

'It's a trick,' he said hoarsely. 'I don't believe you.'

'The police aren't allowed to lie to people they want to question. Do you want to make Linda a widow on top of the shock of finding she's Paterson's daughter?'

Very suddenly several things appeared to happen at once. There was a rending snapping sound and the patter of falling stones. Andrews flung himself flat on the ground and hung over the edge of the cliff, his arms extended downwards. Pollard and Toye simultaneously seized and held him. After an interval which seemed timeless a human voice was telling Grimshaw to put his feet. There was a colossal combined effort as his head and shoulders appeared and he was dragged to safety, collapsing in a dead faint. The mêlée of Pollard, Toye and Andrews disengaged itself.

'A bloody good effort, Andrews,' Pollard said, dusting himself down. 'That split second just saved him.'

'But for you and the Inspector holding on to me I'd have gone with him, sir.'

Toye kneeling by Grimshaw's inert form, glanced up. 'He's coming round, poor blighter.'

'We'll get him into the Rover. Andrews, you drive his car back, will you?'

'Yes, sir.'

Within minutes the two cars had gone, leaving the uninterrupted vast emptiness of the sky and sea and great cliffs, and the distant crash of waves on rock and shingle far below.

177

AFTERMATH

Two Trials

In due course Mark Forbes pleaded 'Not Guilty' in Minstow Crown Court to the charge of wilfully murdering his uncle, John Hamish Paterson of Loyes Cottage, Little Underhill.

James Samson QC opened the case for the Crown by stating the main provision of the Will of Hamish Paterson, the deceased's father. A life interest in his considerable estate, the jury were told, had been left to the deceased with reversion to the defendant. The prosecution maintained that this bequest had led to the cold-blooded and carefully planned murder of John Hamish Paterson by Mark Forbes in October last.

Step by step Samson unfolded a series of events with the assistance of a long succession of witnesses. Among these were a representative of Iremonger Properties, Mrs Dredge, Jim Bagnall, postman, Henry Bull of Grey's Garage, Detective-Inspector Charles Nevinson and Detective-Chief Superintendent of New Scotland Yard. Various sworn statements were handed in as evidence, including one from the Yard's forensic department which had investigated the remains of the shattered windscreen of the defendant's Jaguar.

The defence made stenuous attempts to challenge

178

the prosecution witnesses' statements but with little success. Charles Nevinson, sitting next to Pollard, turned and raised an eyebrow during the second morning of the trial and received an almost imperceptible wink.

Tension in the packed courtroom mounted when Ronald Grimshaw was called by Samson to the witness stand. He had surrendered to his bail and was awaiting his trial as an accessory to John Paterson's murder. He was escorted by two warders and looked pale but composed, giving his wife who was sitting between Bill and Bridget Appleton a quick smile.

In answer to a question from Samson he described how, as he returned from supper with Mr and Mrs Biden of Rosemary Close, a man had come round the side of his house and spoken to him.

'Did you recognise him?' Samson asked.

'Not immediately, but when I switched the porch light on, and he said he was Dr Paterson's nephew, I remembered him coming to the house once before with a message.'

'What reason did he give for his visit on this occasion?'

'He said he wanted my help, and that there was no one else he knew in Minstow. Dr Paterson had slipped and fallen on the stone floor of his garage, fractured his skull and killed himself. I asked if an ambulance had been sent for, and he said no. He was afraid of being suspected of murdering his uncle to get the family money and wanted to stage an accident. He described his plan about the Caravette, and how I was to drive it to Durnycombe next morning impersonating Dr Paterson. When I refused he threatened to tell my wife that she was Paterson's daughter. I said I knew: Paterson had told me that afternoon. Forbes seemed surprised, and asked if my wife knew. I said no. I suppose I ought to have said yes, but I was rattled and lost my head. He repeated his threat to tell her and I – I agreed to do what he wanted. I knew how my wife would feel about it after the way Paterson had treated me.'

'Thank you, Mr Grimshaw,' Samson said. 'Please go on now to describe exactly what took place on Saturday morning 21, October.'

Starting with his departure from home at half-past eight, Ronald Grimshaw described the sequence of events leading up to his being unobtrusively dropped by Forbes at the foot of Twisterdown, his climb up to the site of the abandoned village and meeting with the Penfolds.

'All this is a pack of damned lies,' Forbes suddenly shouted from the dock. I never went near his bloody house.'

He was restrained by the warders and severely rebuked by the judge.

'Have you any further questions to put to this witness, Mr Samson?' the latter asked.

'Only one, my lord. Mr Grimshaw, how do you account for the fact that a pair of spectacles, identified by Mr Woolmer of this city as having been made for you, was found in the pocket of a windcheater belonging to the deceased which was loose in the Caravette?'

'I had to – to wear it,' Ronald Grimshaw replied with an obvious effort. 'On the drive to Durnycombe. I always use spectacles for driving, and automatically take them off when I get out of the car and put them in my pocket. I suppose I did it automatically then. I took off the windcheater and threw it into the Caravette before, well, the next step . . .'

During a sustained attack by counsel for the defence on Ronald Grimshaw's evidence Charles Nevinson pushed a piece of paper towards Pollard. 'So what?' it

180

enquired. Pollard returned it with the additional enquiry
'So when?'

Ronald Grimshaw was followed on the witness stand
by Jean Naylor. The necessity for her testimony had
obliged the prosecution to call her, but not without
misgivings as to how she would stand up to the ordeal. In
the event these proved unfounded. On two occasions
the judge advised counsel for the defence to word his
questions to her more simply, but she clung doggedly to
her basic statement. She had opened a letter to Mrs Ross
from Harringtons which said somebody called John
Hamish Paterson was Linda Grimshaw's father, and she
had told Mark Forbes when he came to stay at Lodwick
last July. Finally she was allowed to stand down, and the
judge adjourned the court for the lunch recess.

Nevinson's and Pollard's speculations were answered
when it reassembled, and counsel for the defence rose to
announce that Mark Forbes requested permission to
change his plea to one of 'Guilty'.

After scathing comments from the judge on greed,
ruthless disregard for human life and exceptionally
abhorrent blackmail, he received a prison sentence of
twenty years accompanied by a recommendation that he
should serve a minimum of fifteen. He was also
reminded that he had forfeited his inheritance.

'It is a principle of the criminal law,' the judge
reminded the court, 'that a man shall not profit from his
crime.'

On the following day Ronald Grimshaw pleaded
'Guilty' to a charge of having committed an offence
under the Criminal Law Act 1967 section 4(1) which
makes it an offence to assist a person guilty of an
arrestable offence. He admitted under questioning that

181

he had not believed Mark Forbes's story of a fatal accidental fall by John Paterson.

The judge addressed him at some length on the seriousness of his offence. He had attempted to pervert the course of justice and was guilty of a criminal contempt of Court. He had, however been subjected to a particularly vicious type of blackmail involving a third and wholly innocent party, his wife.

'I have given all these matters the most careful consideration,' his lordship continued, 'and have come to the conclusion that a suspended sentence of three years is appropriate, also bearing in mind that the defendant's professional career must be assumed to be at an end.'

Further Light through Glass

The Paterson case had attracted wide public interest, and Pollard received numerous accolades including an unexpectedly warm one from his AC. He was careful to ensure that Charles Nevinson received his due share for his invaluable preliminary work, especially as it had finally been decided not to include the letter bomb incident in the charge against Mark Forbes. Absolutely conclusive proof that he had sent it had not been forthcoming.

Among many congratulatory letters to Pollard there had been one marked 'Personal'. It was from Grizel Ross. In the impeccable and slightly formal language of an educated woman of her generation she thanked him for all that he had done to bring the case to what she felt was a right or proper conclusion.

'If you ever find yourself in these parts,' she said, 'it would be a pleasure to me to meet you again.'

A year later this unexpected situation arose.

'She may not even be alive by now,' Pollard objected to Jane, having discovered that he had to go to Northshire in connection with his current case.

'Why not ring and find out?' Jane suggested.

He did so. Grizel Ross herself answered the telephone, her voice instantly recognisable.

'Chief Superintendent Pollard? Well, well,' he heard. 'What a delightful surprise! Could you have luncheon with me here next Tuesday? . . . Pressure of time? . . . I quite understand . . . I'll expect you for a cup of coffee at 11 o'clock, then . . .'

He saw no perceptible change in her. If anything she looked younger and more vital.

'We'll cut the cackle, shall we, as your time is limited,' she said, handing him his coffee. 'I expect you would be interested to hear how things have turned out.'

Pollard assured her that he would.

'Well, Linda and Ron – I've managed to get used to the appalling abbreviation of his name – have a nice little cottage here in Lodwick. No, I didn't buy it for them. It was paid for out of the proceeds of the sale of their Minstow house. I felt strongly from the first that they must have a sense of independence. At the moment Linda is the breadwinner. On my advice she took a secretarial refresher course and is an efficient peripatetic farm secretary on four days each week. Ron is working on an archaelogical excavation of a Roman camp ten miles from here. The work is unpaid but he gets his keep from Monday to Friday each week. So they are the right way round. Linda was always the stronger personality who ought to be in the lead. Ron is enjoying the hard dirty work, and I am quietly manoeuvering behind the scenes to get him a permanent job with the Northshire Archaelogical Society, so that he'll be employed all the year round, winter as well as summer. Have another cup of coffee, won't you?'

Accepting a second cup, Pollard asked how the Grimshaws were fitting into Lodwick.

'Very happily. There was a lot of local sympathy for them both, and the fact that they buckled to and showed no sign of living on me told in their favour. People are very independent in these parts, you know. Incidentally I have legally adopted Linda. You see, Chief Superintendent, it turned out that she wasn't John Paterson's daughter after all.'

Pollard sat looking at her in dumbfounded silence.

'It was like this,' Grizel Ross went on. 'I have kept a diary from an early age: there are seventy-three little leather-bound volumes in a bookcase in my bedroom. I often dip into them before I settle down for the night. Last August – 1st August, 1984 – Linda and I celebrated our joint birthday: her twenty-eighth and my eighty-fourth. In bed that night I picked out my diary for the year of her birth, 1956, and looked up 1st August. The only entry for that day was that my brother Hamish had driven down to Southampton to meet John on his return from the United States. He had held a junior lectureship over there for a year, and taken the opportunity of visiting places of geological interest like the Grand Canyon. Quite suddenly the significance of this dawned on me. Over the next few days I worked steadily through the 1955 diary. Rather a strain on my elderly eyes as the ink had faded in places, but that magnifying glass over there that you yourself used on your previous visit was a great help. And the upshot of my researches was this, Chief Superintendent. Hamish had seen John off from Southampton on 31 August 1955, and John had not once returned to Britain until 1 August 1956, the day Linda was born. In short, he could not have been her father.'

184

'Why do you think he apparently accepted the fact that he was?' Pollard asked.

'Undoubtedly he had a casual sexual relationship with her mother while on one of his visits to Wringtonford in connection with the family works. Probably not long before leaving for America. I imagine that he was a cut above the poor girl's usual clientele, and when she subsequently became pregnant by another man she indulged in the fantasy that John was the father. John's sense of moral responsibility was minimal where his personal convenience was concerned, and I don't suppose he gave the girl another thought.'

'Have you told Linda?' Pollard asked.

'I told both Linda and Ron. It was rather moving. You see, they were fond enough of each other to accept the original situation, but their joy on learning the truth is something that I shall always remember. You see, reverting to my adoption of Linda, it was a sorrow to my husband and myself that we had no children, and he was unwilling to consider adopting any. But now the decision is mine, and I have a legal, if not a lineal daughter. And,' she looked across at Pollard and smiled, 'there'll be a legal grandson or grandaughter in the autumn.'

Pollard returned her smile with warmth and genuine admiration.

'Possibly both, Mrs Ross,' he said. 'My wife and I would strongly recommend assorted twins.'

185

If you have enjoyed this book and would like to receive details of other Walker mystery titles, please write to:

Mystery Editor
Walker and Company
720 Fifth Avenue
New York, NY 10019